EDWARDIAN DRAMA

EDWARDIAN DRAMA
A Critical Study

Ian Clarke

faber and faber
LONDON · BOSTON

First published in 1989
by Faber and Faber Limited
3 Queen Square London WC1N 3AU

Phototypeset by Wilmaset Birkenhead Wirral
Printed in Great Britain by
Richard Clay Ltd Bungay Suffolk

British Library Cataloguing in Publication Data is available.

ISBN 0–571–14892–1

In an age when critical theory promises, or threatens, to 'cross over' into literature and to become its own object of study, there is a powerful case for re-asserting the primacy of the literary text. These studies are intended in the first instance to provide substantial critical introductions to writers of major importance. Although each contributor inevitably writes from a considered critical position, it is not the aim of the series to impose a uniformity of theoretical approach. Each book will make use of biographical material and each will conclude with a select bibliography which will in all cases take note of the latest developments usefully relevant to the subject. Beyond that, however, contributors have been chosen for their critical abilities as well as for their familiarity with the subject of their choice.

Although the primary aim of the series is to focus attention on individual writers, there will be exceptions. And although the majority of writers or periods studied will be of the twentieth century, this is not intended to preclude other writers or periods. Above all, the series aims to return readers to a sharpened awareness of those texts without which there would be no criticism.

John Lucas

For
Julie
and
in memory of
Elizabeth Potts
(1892–1987)

Contents

I
Aspects of the Theatrical Context

Hierarchically and organizationally the commercial Edwardian theatre was dominated by the actor managers. They leased and managed the building, chose the plays and controlled their production, and usually acted a leading role. A consequence of the extent of this organizational control was an ability throughout the period to embody and create the tone of the theatre as a social institution. They epitomized an upper-middle-class conception of the theatre which was espoused not only by themselves, the purveyors of the drama, but also by the patrons of the theatre. Thus they aimed to project an idealized vision of upper-middle-class decorum, suavity, and, notwithstanding the facts of their private lives, irreproachable respectability. In the images they created, both on and off the stage, they presented a construction of Edwardian experience which was suitably flattering and acceptable to the bulk of the theatre-going public. Despite the image-making, the social image was partly founded on fact. For much of the nineteenth century, the acting profession had not genuinely been received into polite society, but, by the Edwardian age, it had so successfully been assimilated into the recognized social hierarchy that those at the top of the profession, the actor managers, were liberally bestowed with knighthoods for their services to the theatre. Henry Irving, Squire Bancroft, Charles Wyndham, John Hare, Herbert Beerbohm Tree, Johnston Forbes Robertson and George Alexander, all received such honours in the late Victorian and Edwardian period. This relatively new-found social position and respectability affected a whole range of basic assumptions about the nature and function of the theatre as an institution and about the drama it presented.

An insight into these assumptions is provided by Walter Macqueen-Pope's recollections of the Edwardian theatre, *Carriages at*

Eleven. His account is so partial and nostalgic that its objective accuracy is seriously called into question. However, the real value of the book lies in the fact that its own commentary comprises an unequivocal endorsement of the social and ideological basis of the Edwardian commercial theatre. Macqueen-Pope's tone, in keeping with his vision of his subject matter, is smug and self-congratulatory and he provides an unashamed compendium of a whole range of social snobberies and prejudices. He applauds a concept of the theatre which accords with notions of appropriate behaviour and taste: 'It was run as were the homes of the people, with stately decorum and good manners. It had distinction with stability, and this was bestowed upon it by the actor-managers, whose theatres were their homes' (p. 8). It is not difficult to decode who, as far as Macqueen-Pope is concerned, constituted *the people.* The etiquette he proposes is patently a correlative of affluence and superior social class. Nevertheless, the image was a powerful one and was a creation of the development of the theatre in a latter part of the nineteenth century.

The management of the Bancrofts at the Prince of Wales's during the 1860s, with the introduction of rosebud chintz in the circle and carpeting in the stalls, is viewed by theatre historians as a watershed in initiating the provision of theatre as a social event deliberately aimed at the middle classes. Throughout the rest of the century new theatre building and the extensive refurbishment of existing buildings was committed, in the more expensive parts of the house, to increasingly greater opulence and elegance, and the comfort of the spectator was further enhanced by improvements in the lighting, heating and ventilation of the auditorium. The keyword to the experience of visiting fashionable theatres during the late Victorian and Edwardian period is gentility. The prospectus of the rebuilding of Her Majesty's which opened in 1897 shows that these requirements were fulfilled:

> On the ground floor, level with the street, will be found Orchestral Stalls, Pit Stalls and the Pit.
> The first floor will be devoted to the Dress Circle and Family

Circle. The second tier consists of the Upper Circle, Amphitheatre and the Gallery behind.

The five doorways in the centre of the Haymarket facade underneath the loggia open into a vestibule exclusively for the use of the two classes of the Stalls and the Dress and Family Circles, and the Stalls have a third way out, level with the pavement in Charles Street . . .

The style adopted for the auditorium of the theatre is Louis XIV. There are private boxes on each of the tiers adjoining the proscenium and separated from it and other parts of the auditorium by marble columns. The hangings are of cerise-coloured embroidered silk and the walls generally are covered with a paper of the same tone.

The seating for Stalls, Dress and Family Circles is in arm chairs, covered with velvet the same colour as the curtains.

The Tableau curtains are of velvet of a similar tone behind which is the Act Drop of tapestry copied from one of the Gobelin Tapestries now in Paris.

The whole of the theatre and annexes are lighted by the Electric Light taken from three centres, so that should any one centre fail, the other systems are always available. Hanging from the ceiling is a cut glass and brass electrolier and brackets of Louis XIV style are fixed round the box fronts and on the side walls. (Mander and Mitchenson, p. 113)

The very start of the evening's entertainment at eight o'clock or after, some two hours later than earlier in the nineteenth century, fitted in with middle-class eating habits. People could dine in the comfort of their own homes before spending an evening possibly in even greater comfort and splendour at the theatre.

Some commentators, in this case Mario Borsa, did not share Macqueen-Pope's enthusiastic approval of the tone of the theatre and the social images it promoted:

Thither do the Briton and his womankind resort, arrayed in full evening panoply, in calm expectation of a reception befitting the guests of a peer's drawing-room, rather than the patrons of a place of public entertainment . . . The entire organization of the theatre reflects that special and aristocratic conception of its status which is the point of view of its patrons. (p. 279)

Henry James was another wry observer of the nature of this after-dinner entertainment:

In the house itself everything seems to contribute to the impression . . . that the theatre in England is a social luxury and not an artistic necessity . . . [The audience] is well dressed, tranquil, motionless; it suggests domestic virtue and comfortable homes; it looks as if it had come to the play in its own carriage, after a dinner of beef and pudding. (pp. 100–1)

The architecture of the theatre building and its internal arrangements, as evidenced by the new Her Majesty's, promoted a rigid system of class stratification, the principles of which receive Macqueen-Pope's full approbation:

If by reason of your social standing, or your purse (and in Edwardian days this was becoming almost the same thing) you occupied the boxes, stalls or dress circle, you wore evening dress. You would not have dreamt of doing otherwise – and if you had, you would not have been admitted. If you were a still honoured, but not top-table guest, well, there was the pit or the gallery to suit your pocket and your wardrobe, or that curious, class-conscious part of the house, the upper circle, for what might be described as the lower middle class of playgoers. (p. 9)

The conservatism of the theatre's class-consciousness reflected what was comforting to the sensibility not only of many Edwardian playgoers but to playgoers of the 1860s who encountered that vision of the class system provided by the honest working man Sam Gerridge in Robertson's *Caste* (1867): 'People should stick to their own class. Life's a railway journey, and Mankind's a passenger – first class, second class, third class. Any person found riding in a superior class to that for which he has taken his ticket will be removed at the first station stopped at, according to the bye-laws of the company' (Act 1). Social segregation in the theatres was augmented by separate entrances and public areas for the various sections of seating, and this segregation was most fully implemented by a graduated pricing policy. Prices of admission were comparable in the fashionable theatres and remained constant throughout the period. Those for Wyndham's which opened in 1899 are typical: Stalls, 10s. 6d.; Dress Circle, 7s. and 5s.; Family Circle, 4s.; Pit, 2s. 6d.; Gallery, 1s. The most expensive seats effectively excluded those not moderately wealthy; but the cheapest areas would not have disbarred those with considerably smaller incomes. The dominant social tone of the theatre is a correlative of the furnishing and fitting of the more expensive parts of the house. This is clearly where the actor managers derived their greatest satisfaction and, probably more importantly, their self-validation. It also dominates the commentary of observers like Macqueen-Pope, Borsa, and Henry James. But in terms of the whole theatre building and the class composition of the audience, it is only part of the story.

Nevertheless, the tone of the Edwardian commercial theatre, with its concern for the preservation of social hierarchy, encouraged the presentation of a certain sort of play which Bernard Shaw described in the Preface to *Three Plays for Puritans*. The manager, he observed, was ultimately uninterested in whether a play was good or bad so long as it was 'nice', 'nice plays, with nice dresses, nice drawing-rooms and nice people are indispensable: to be ungenteel is worse than to fail' (*The Bodley Head Bernard Shaw*, II, p. 21; hereafter this edition will be abbreviated as *B H S*). This demand for 'nice dresses' and 'nice drawing-rooms' encouraged the presentation of a certain sort of spectacle in the drama; 'nice people' dress nicely and move in suitably nice surroundings. The tinsel and glitter of historical costume drama and archaeologically accurate Shakespeare provided the visual spectacle which enchanted Edwardian audiences. But the provision of a similar gratification in the serious realistic drama of modern life became what is essentially an issue of social class and resulted in a marked tendency for the staging of plays which dealt solely with the upper reaches of society. Only in that area of modern life could the setting and costuming satisfy the desire for gentility and the visually 'nice'.

In the drama of modern life, the actor manager could only truly cut a suitably fine figure by representing characters from the higher sections of society. The demonstrable class-consciousness of the theatre as an institution, which the actor manager at its head fostered and in part created, demanded that he should represent on stage a reflection of the social status of the highest section of the audience or the highest point to which it could reasonably aspire. The appropriateness of this image was shared both by the actor manager and his audience; Harley Granville Barker illustrated how this expectation determined the class structure of the drama:

> The actor-manager had then to be reckoned with, who, what-ever his artistic virtues, did not see himself, and simply could not have let his faithful audiences see him side-whiskered, reach-me-down suited, with pepper-and-salt trousers slightly baggy at the knee. In the popular play, too, pretty ladies must parade in smart frocks, half a dozen at least, and as many more as the playwright could provide for and the management afford. Women went to the theatre as much for the dresses as the drama; they must have their money's worth. Not the lowest of the barriers between Ibsen and the 'recognized' London theatre was the distressing fact that there is hardly a fashiona-bly dressed woman to be found in his plays. Hedda Gabler, to be sure; but heaven help us, even she *walks* home after a party! (Barker, 1930, p. 166)

No carriages at eleven for Hedda Gabler. Even if Ibsen's morality and subject matter had been acceptable, his depiction of the Norwegian bourgeoisie was sufficiently removed from the setting of fashionable society to provoke from Clement Scott the damn-ing epithet 'suburban'. Scott's positions as drama critic of the *Daily Telegraph* and editor of *The Theatre* provided him an influential platform, and his criticism, in this instance, is of value precisely because it expressed the feeling of a large section of the Edwardian playgoing public. The result was the predomination of a drama whose subject matter was socially restricted to the lives of the upper middle classes — the society drama. It was a drama which, in its subject matter, would concur with the social tone of the theatre as an institution.

But for the society dramatists the choice of subject matter was more than a question of taste. Arthur Wing Pinero believed there was a necessary conjunction between a drama possessed of a coherent and weighty intellectual order and the depiction of higher social classes:

> I think you would find, if you wanted to write drama, not only that wealth and leisure are more productive of dramatic complications than hard work, but that if you want to get a certain order of ideas expressed or questions discussed, you must go pretty well up in the social scale . . . You must take into account the inarticulateness, the inexpressiveness, of the English lower-middle and lower classes – their reluctance to analyse, to generalise, to give vivid utterance either to their thoughts or their emotions. (Archer, 1904, pp. 21–2)

Henry Arthur Jones, similarly, believed that a play would be more likely to attain the status of literature, which was its continual goal, if it were 'a vehicle for memorable and distinguished conversation' (Cordell, p. 198) and therefore peopled by those who can supply such conversation. These assumptions are based on the idea that the expression of a worthwhile body of ideas is dependent upon a set of linguistic acquisitions – articulateness, formality, abstraction – which are seen primarily as a prerogative of the upper classes. There is a further implicit assumption, far from unique to the late Victorian and Edwardian period, that memorable and distinguished conversations are, like the spectacle of upper-middle-class life itself, pleasurable.

The corollary is that any depiction of the lower social classes is likely to be unpleasurable, unpleasant, and is thus to be avoided. Jones condemned what he called modern pessimistic realistic drama (by which he means what was seen in the 1890s as the school of Ibsen) precisely on these grounds:

> It tried to seduce us from our smug suburban villas into all sorts of gruesome kitchen-middens. Now it really does not matter

what happens in kitchen-middens. The dark places of the earth are full of cruelties and abominations. So are the dark places of the soul. We know that well enough. But the epitaph – it is already written – on all this realistic business will be – 'It does not matter what happens in kitchen-middens.' (H. A. Jones, 1895, p. vii)

Jones acknowledges the existence, but demands the exclusion from the Edwardian theatre, of such things. Shaw, with a typical amount of overstatement, described the effect of such attitudes when transferred to the stage:

Our ideal prosperity is not the prosperity of the industrial north, but the prosperity of the Isle of Wight, of Folkestone and Ramsgate, of Nice and Monte Carlo. That is the only prosperity you see on the stage, where the workers are all footmen, parlourmaids, comic lodging-letters, and fashionable professional men, whilst the heroes and heroines are miraculously provided with unlimited dividends and eat gratuitously, like the knights in Don Quixote's books of chivalry. (*B H S*, II, pp. 515–16)

The Edwardian audiences seemingly found acceptable and palatable a depiction of the dominant class and the results of the wealth of a modern industrial nation, but not a depiction of the things and class which produced that wealth. The aversion was such that Squire Bancroft, a senior and respected actor manager, could say of the satirical whimsy of Barrie's *The Admirable Crichton* (1902), 'It deals . . . with the juxtaposition of the drawing-room and the servants' hall – always to me a very painful subject.' A. E. W. Mason, who recorded the remark, significantly comments, 'It seemed to me that I heard the whole of that era . . . epitomised and defined in that one unexpected sentence' (p. 136).

The desire for 'nice' plays, over and above its creation of a social tone, entailed a more fundamental ideological affiliation. 'Nice' plays could only be those which demonstrated and endorsed a non-objectionable subject matter and morality. The successful plays of the serious commercial theatre were almost inevitably conservative in matters of social conduct and sexual morality. The success of the drama depended not only on a congruity of taste between providers and consumers but on a congruity between the ideological foundations of the Edwardian theatre, ramified by notions of a stable social structure and concepts of correct behaviour, and the ideological construction of the drama itself.

The mediation of moral and social issues on the Edwardian stage was, however, complicated by the appearance of Ibsen in the 1890s. The staging of *A Doll's House* in 1889 and *Hedda Gabler* and *Ghosts* in 1891 produced in many critics a horror at the spectacle of the desecration of their household gods. The horror did not stem, as Harley Granville Barker suggested, from the dearth of fashionably dressed women but because of the offence which Ibsen's work gave to the gentlemanly instincts of the actor manager and his audience. Not only were they cheated of the vindication of their own values and standards, but Ibsen dared to speak of the unmentionable. The spectacle of a woman who could desert her home, husband, and defenceless children (an offence against certain orthodox images of Victorian womanhood), or the depiction of the effects of congenital disease (not a topic of discussion fit for a theatre which took as its model of correct behaviour the upper-middle-class drawing-room) provoked a storm of outraged vilification. The following choice epithets flowed from the pen of Clement Scott – 'an open drain', 'a loathsome sore unbandaged', 'a dirty act done publicly', 'a lazar-house with all its doors and windows open' (Rowell, 1978, p. 129). His hysteria is now justly notorious, but he undoubtedly expressed the feeling of many late Victorians as other contemporary criticism in a similar vein indicates. Scott's imagery is significant. He asserts, as does Jones, not that such things do not exist, but that they are outside the world picture of the Edwardian commercial theatre, that they had been and should continue to be excluded from that world of selective vision.

Although Ibsen was initially promoted under the auspices of the minority theatre, the strength of his impact necessarily had its effect on the commercial stage. Sydney Grundy, stalwart of

Victorian conventionality, acknowledged Ibsen's presence by a direct satiric attack on Ibsen in particular and naturalistic work in general. In *A Bunch of Violets* (1894), Mark Murgatroyd, a plain-spoken Yorkshireman up in London, reads of a theatrical 'master-piece' and goes to see it as he feels 'in the mood for a good laugh'; not surprisingly he comes away disappointed:

> Hero was suffering from some brain complaint . . . and his wife didn't like it: so she got making eyes at husband's doctor, but that came to nowt, for he had something the matter wi' his ancestors. Well they were seen philandering by t'owd mother, but that came to nowt, for she was paralyzed and couldn't tell tales. Then wife and doctor shoot one another – husband shoots himself – and t'auld girl's left alone wi' the three corpses. (Act 1)

Grundy's statement unwittingly indicates that the advanced drama had its own conventions and dramatic devices, its own ways of constructing images of reality. But other dramatists were necessarily more subtle in their acknowledgement of Ibsen's impact. Avoiding Grundy's hostile satire, they inaugurated a process of assimilation. Shaw analysed the dilemma facing managers and dramatists alike: 'In short, a modern manager need not produce The Wild Duck; but he must be very careful not to produce a play which will seem insipid and old-fashioned to playgoers who have seen The Wild Duck, even though they may have hissed it' (Shaw, 1932, I, p. 165).

What resulted was a compromise between the outspokenness of Ibsen, which audiences found objectionable, and the conventional realistic play to which they were accustomed. The chronology of the appearance in 1893 of Pinero's first fully formulated serious problem play, *The Second Mrs Tanqueray*, after the productions of Ibsen's work in England in 1889 and 1891 is an illustration of this tendency. Pinero's play shows not a direct Ibsenite influence but an extension of tone and subject matter which the appearance of Ibsen contributed towards bringing about. *The Second Mrs Tanqueray* is typical of many plays of the period in that it is ultimately a conventionally moral play with a veneer of something that faintly echoed Ibsen in its apparent compassionate treatment of serious social and moral issues. Whilst appearing to be progressive, this sort of play was successful because it was not too far ahead of public opinion and consequently not too offensive to the audience or the actor manager.

Yet whilst their ideological centres may be ultimately supportive of dominant codes, in the context of the Edwardian theatre the plays often seemed to sail close to the wind. There was always the danger that they would stray from the daring to the offensive. Jones intended that the eponymous heroine of *The Case of Rebellious Susan* (1894) should pay back her husband's adultery in its own kind. He claimed, 'I made very sure that she did, but the actor was a bit delicate with his audiences and refused to utter a few lines that made it clear' (Cordell, p. 216). Wyndham objected not to his own lines but to those of his leading lady Mary Moore. The line in which he required a change indicates not only the extent of his delicacy but just how tactful Jones had been in the first place in making the fact clear to the audience. Wyndham suggested the line 'Oh, I should kill myself if anyone knew! You have never spoken of me – boasted to any of your men friends – ?' (Act 2) should simply become 'You have never spoken of me to any of your men friends?' Wyndham's correspondence about the matter in turn asserts absolutist ethical stances, questions of good taste, and commercial considerations. Typical of the style promoted by the very role of *raisonneur* that Jones provided for him, Wyndham added, 'I am not speaking as a moralist, I am simply voicing the public instinct' (D. A. Jones, p. 166). Wendy Trewin (p. 133) argues that Wyndham's and Mary Moore's personal situation (she was in a discreet but illicit relationship with Wyndham) made them especially sensitive to imputations on her reputation from the role she represented on stage. Mary Moore was not alone in this perception of the relationship between the moral standing of a fictional character and the performer who represented it. Evelyn Millard, recently married, recognized an indelicacy in being required to utter the line 'I swear to you by my unborn child' in Jones's *The Lackey's Carnival*

(1900) and felt obliged to abandon the role of heroine. Even Lena Ashwell, active in the cause of advanced drama and prominent in the Actresses' Franchise League, felt uneasy about playing the lead in *Mrs Dane's Defence* (1900): 'I was a dark horse, and Mrs Dane was a woman with a murky past, and heroines should have virtue on their side. Even if for a time circumstances were against them, they should be proved innocent in the end' (W. Trewin, p. 153). The actor managers, concerned as they were with their social status and the proprietorship of their theatres as their homes, were not inclined to present plays of modern life which showed them in roles that seemed to condone the unfitting or the indecorous. It was for them only natural to take as a moral reference point the role of characters who affirmed the dominant morality – that of the upper middle class.

In their defence, it can however be said that the actor managers were not necessarily pandering to the philistine taste of a self-satisfied and self-congratulatory audience. Their artistic standards, as they deemed them, were high. And although they were in many ways satisfying their own view of themselves and the function of their theatre, they did effectively consolidate the reputation of the theatre. Their reduction of the length of the programme to, most typically, a short curtain-raiser and one full-length piece presented in an atmosphere of decorous behaviour implicitly asserted that, whatever its merits or demerits, the play itself was to be treated with respect and could be taken seriously.

But however contented large numbers of late Victorian and Edwardian playgoers, performers, and managers were with the social and ideological constructs of the commercial theatre and the drama it promoted, from the late 1880s the dissatisfied voices of certain literary figures and drama critics began to make themselves heard. These included most notably William Archer, George Moore, Henry James, George Bernard Shaw, and A. B. Walkley; one of the most persistent voices belonged to a Dutchman J. T. Grein. In 1887 Grein published in his journal *The Weekly Comedy* what amounted to a manifesto calling for the opening of the stage to 'all who have something new to say, who have the courage and the ability to cast aside banal sentiment, faulty construction, and useless padding, when writing for the stage' (Woodfield, p. 176). Throughout the 1890s the dissentient voices argued for a widening of the range and methods of the commercial drama and for an expansion of the restrictions of its subject matter and ideological assumptions. In effect they argued for different modes of dramatic writing. They found their initial model in continental European naturalism and the work of Ibsen, Zola, and Tolstoy, in comparison to which, they believed, the efforts of contemporary English playwrights were little more than facile. It was recognized by those arguing for what was perceived as the new or advanced drama that the inherent conservatism of the commercial theatre would be antagonistic to it. Consequently it would be a minority not a popular drama nor could it be accommodated to or by the commercial theatre. It would require for its staging different forms of theatrical organization – a minority not a commercial theatre. They found their theatrical model in André Antoine's Théâtre Libre established in Paris in 1887.

Grein inaugurated the Independent Theatre Society in London with a production of Ibsen's *Ghosts* at the Royalty in 1891. *Ghosts* had been staged by the Théâtre Libre the previous year and was staged later in 1891 as the opening production of Otto Brahm's *Die Freie Bühne* in Berlin. Grein's choice of *Ghosts* placed the Independent Theatre Society in a wider European context and asserted that the conventions of literary naturalism were one of the appropriate modes of serious contemporary dramatic writing. By its demise in 1898 Grein's Independent Theatre had staged other works by Ibsen and plays by Zola and Brieux. But the range of its productions, which included plays by Webster, Shakespeare, Browning, Maeterlinck, and Arthur Symons, was an indication that the minority theatre movement would not restrict itself to contemporary or naturalistic works.

From the 1890s to the end of the period several other ventures developed which were committed predominantly to the staging of non-commercial drama. These ventures fall into two major groups. The play-producing societies (the Independent Theatre Society, the New Century Theatre, 1898, and the Stage Society,

1899) offered occasional productions of plays and, having no permanent theatre of their own, relied on the support of sympathetic managers and lessees for the use of a number of theatres to stage their work. The other group differed in that a management would take over a specific theatre and operate short-run or repertory seasons. The most significant of these were the seasons of Granville Barker and J. E. Vedrenne at the Court, 1904–7, and at the Savoy, 1907–8. Following their example, seasons at other London theatres were attempted, most notably that of Charles Frohman at the Duke of York's in 1910. Equally important to the promotion of the new drama was the establishment of regional repertory theatres, most significantly at Manchester in 1908, Glasgow, 1909, Liverpool, 1911, Birmingham, 1913. Despite their differences they each provided a theatrical organization based on very different assumptions from those of the commercial theatre.

The relationship between the commercial theatre and the minority ventures consists of a series of complex interfaces and overlaps. Although it is convenient and indeed necessary to make a distinction between the two areas of theatrical activity, the distinction can in some respects be no more than a sort of shorthand. The commercial and minority theatres were by no means totally discrete and their lines of demarcation were often blurred. It was not uncommon for the same theatre buildings and the same actors and actresses, either as performers or managers, to be associated with both the commercial and the minority theatres. Similarly individual plays, seemingly the property of the minority theatre, could cross boundaries. If sufficiently successful they could become a viable proposition for a commercial management. Yet by the end of the period, as can be seen from the statistical postscript to this chapter, it was only Shaw's work which had managed to make any real inroad into the commercial stage.

Nevertheless the early play-producing societies announced from the very start the minority theatre's consciousness of its role in providing an alternative to the drama of the commercial theatre. The Independent Theatre Society aimed to give 'performances of plays which have a literary and artistic rather than a commercial value' (Nicoll, 1973, p. 52). The Stage Society originated from a similar desire 'to secure the production of plays of obvious power and merit which lacked, under the conditions then prevalent on the stage, any opportunity for their presentation' (Incorporated Stage Society, p. 7), and the aim of the New Century Theatre was to stage 'plays of intrinsic interest which find no place on the stage in the ordinary way of theatrical business' (Woodfield, pp. 56–7). What is intimated in each statement is that the drama staged by the play-producing societies would not be circumscribed by the commercial necessity which governed the established London theatre. As Bernard Shaw said of the Independent Theatre, its most essential independence was that it was 'independent of commercial success' (Shaw, 1932, I, p. 19). It is far from the truth to suggest that all managers or dramatists of the commercial theatre were unprepared to take risks in the interests of their art. Nevertheless, the established theatre was bound by the exigencies of commerce; the managements could not affort to stage plays that would not pay and dramatists could not afford to write plays that the managements would not accept. The play-producing societies were freed from such exigencies precisely because their avowed aim was not profit. They operated as private societies financially dependent not on box-office takings but predominantly on the subscriptions of their members.

Perhaps the single most important advantage accruing from their status as societies was their ability to circumvent the dictates of the censor. Since 1737 the Lord Chamberlain's Office had been granted the unfettered right to ban any play from public performance. The Theatre Regulation Act of 1843 emphasized that prohibition should be exercised when the Lord Chamberlain (or more precisely his Examiner of Plays) 'shall be of the opinion that it is fitting for the preservation of good manners, decorum or of the public peace so to do'. The Examiner addressed himself with particular vigilance to religious, political, and moral matters which challenged current orthodoxies. The minority theatre movement provided a focal point for opposition throughout the late Victorian and Edwardian period to restrictions placed upon the stage by an official beyond democratic or legal redress. The choice of *Ghosts*, which the then Examiner is reported as refusing even to consider granting a licence, as the first Independent Theatre Society production was a provocative statement of principle. An invaluable service was rendered by presenting, if only to a limited audience, a play which could not legally be shown otherwise. The Stage Society would provide a similar service to other proscribed pieces including Shaw's *Mrs Warren's Profession* (1902) and Granville-Barker's *Waste* (1907).

In addition to providing a stage for plays which would not otherwise be presented, another aim of the minority theatre was to find and encourage new dramatists. One aim of the Stage Society expressed a common attitude: 'The most important function of the Society has been, and must continue to be, the search for new playwrights' (Incorporated Stage Society, p. 8). The Independent Theatre Society depended heavily on continental European writers for suitable plays. The only notable plays by British authors were Shaw's *Widowers' Houses* (1892) and George Moore's *The Strike at Arlingford* (1893). By the early years of the twentieth century the Stage Society, whilst continuing to stage foreign drama, was beginning to indicate that there were new British playwrights producing work which could appropriately be promoted by the minority theatre. By 1904 it had featured plays by Somerset Maugham, St John Hankin, and Gilbert Murray's translation of *Andromache*; it had staged Granville Barker's *The Marrying of Ann Leete* (1902) and, intimations of things to come, five plays by Shaw: *You Never Can Tell* (1899), *Candida* (1900), *Captain Brassbound's Conversion* (1900), *Mrs Warren's Profession*, and *The Admirable Bashville* (1903).

The work of the Stage Society and, to a lesser extent, of the Independent Theatre Society and the New Century Theatre was consolidated in 1904 by the inauguration of the management of Vedrenne and Barker at the Court. The three seasons were a remarkable achievement. A total of 988 performances of thirty-two plays by seventeen authors were presented. Of these a mere five plays were by modern European dramatists and they accounted for only thirty-seven of the performances. Gilbert

Murray's versions of Euripides' *Electra, Hippolytus*, and *The Trojan Women* accounted for forty-eight. Shaw's dominance of the seasons, eleven plays and 701 performances, earned the enterprise the reputation of being a Shavian repertory. The Court was crucial to the establishing of Shaw's reputation; the success of his plays crucial to the success of the Court. Only by operating a short-run system could the Court, and other later ventures, present plays, and therefore provide opportunities for new writers, in such numbers. The commercial constraints of the established theatre required long runs and revivals of past successes; the commercial theatre could not hope to match the opportunities for new work offered by the Court.

The organizational significance of the Vedrenne–Barker seasons, as opposed to the play-producing societies, lay in their permanent home and the greater regularity and continuity of performance. The success or failure of the enterprise would depend primarily on box-office takings, not on membership subscriptions. Unlike the societies, the Court seasons competed in the same marketplace as the commercial theatres. But they could hardly hope to compete on the same terms. Though the Court seasons made a small profit, this was made possible by a paring down of expenses to a minimum and the eschewing of the lavish production values of the commercial stage. In addition, performers had to be sufficiently committed to the venture to be prepared to give their services for fees much smaller than they could have commanded in the commercial theatre. However, the season at the Savoy (1907–8) mounted by Vedrenne and Barker could not manage the minimal financial success of the Court seasons. It ended in debt and severed the partnership of the managers. Charles Frohman mounted an ambitious repertory season of ten plays (including Galsworthy's *Strife*, Shaw's *Misalliance*, Granville Barker's *The Madras House* and his collaboration with Housman, *Prunella*) at the Duke of York's in 1910. This venture was also a financial failure. Frohman, an American impresario with a good track record of making money out of the commercial theatre on both sides of the Atlantic, was an unlikely supporter of the minority drama. That in itself makes his involvement significant. He may have miscalculated the financial chances of his venture, but his commitment shows that he believed there was at least some commercial potential in the minority drama. Even so, he must have known that the profits from a repertory of minority drama could not approach those of his earlier strictly commercial activities. The artistic credit to be acquired by association with the venture was a major consideration. Some twenty years after the vilification which had accompanied the first production of the Independent Theatre Society, promotion of the new drama could be respectable and prestigious. Frohman lost heavily over the seventeen weeks of the season and was probably grateful for the fact that the King's death in May gave a pretext for terminating the venture.

The reasons for the financial failure of the ventures at the Savoy and the Duke of York's are complex. Yet the failure is indicative of the minority theatre's more general inability to achieve a financial viability without either subsidy or the strict curtailment of expenses. Shaw, in a letter to Barker about the Frohman season, claimed 'all we have succeeded in doing is to prove the impossibility of a high class theatre under a commercial management' (Shaw, 1957, p. 165). Barker concurred; the Duke of York's had shown that 'a Repertory Theatre cannot be made to pay in the commercial sense of the word' (Barker, 1910, p. 639). What was undeniably true was that the economics of London theatre management militated against short-run and repertory operation. Shaw's *Arms and the Man*, for instance played at the Avenue in 1894 for seventy-five performances. A run of that length in the late Victorian theatre would normally indicate a relatively successful production. Yet Shaw's own account of the financial return on the play tells a somewhat different story: 'To witness it the public paid £1777:5:6, an average of £23:2:5 per representation (including nine matinées). A publisher receiving £1700 for a book would have made a satisfactory profit: experts in West End theatrical management will contemplate that figure with a grim smile' (*B H S* I, p. 372). An actor manager like George Alexander might have smiled indeed. *The Second Mrs Tanqueray*, which opened in 1893, ran for 223 performances. The money paid to see it amounted the £36,688 13s.; this represents an average per performance in excess of £164. The most successful collaboration of a Pinero play and Alexander's management was *His House in Order* (1906). The run was 428 performances, the receipts were £78,189 12s., the average per performance was in excess of £182. The commercially successful play was an extremely valuable commodity. By 1914 the personal profit accruing to Alexander as actor manager from the initial run, revivals, and provincial tours of *The Second Mrs Tanqueray* amounted to more than £21,000 and of *His House in Order* £35,000. (These two sums include the salary of roughly £80 a week Alexander paid himself for acting in his own productions.) Then, as now, the shibboleths of commerce and profit in an unsubsidized theatre argued for long runs and large audiences as the only hope of defraying the heavy expense of play production.

The crucial question, inextricably linked with the failure to attain financial viability, is why it was that the drama of the minority theatre remained a minority taste. One answer lies in the organization of the minority theatre ventures. A repertory or short-run system disturbed established theatrical habits. The long run was a part of a wider sense of stability promoted by the commercial theatre. Audiences needed time to become accustomed to new habits, not least of which was that a short run was not concomitant with a play's failure. They had to come to appreciate new sorts of theatrical language. New production styles and values were often not just economic necessities but a deliberate rejection of the elaborate representational literalism of the tradition of Victorian staging. What the audiences saw on stage could refute a very simple expectation of what a play should look like.

Similarly the plays presented under the auspices of the minority ventures frequently made new demands on their audience. The unfamiliar modes of Euripides' tragedy, Maeterlinck's symbolist drama, or what were seen as the overlong discussion plays of Shaw and Granville Barker, were not easily assimilated by an audience accustomed to the offerings of the commercial stage. Plays which were seemingly closer to the dominant realist mode, *Ghosts* being the first and most notorious example, often offended by their subject matter and ideological position. The drama was perceived as gloomy, pessimistic, morbid; it was commonly held that a play presented by a minority theatre venture would axiomatically be of amateurish construction and unpleasant theme. That prerequisite of a drama's popularity, subscribed to by the commercial stage, whereby the drama vindicates good taste and dominant ideological assumptions was lacking, and often quite deliberately so, in the minority theatre.

The nature of the minority drama presupposed an audience with both a different ideological bias and different intellectual interests from those which found validation and gratification in the commercial drama. The common satirical imputation of the traditionalist point of view was that the audience was comprised of faddists bent on sermons rather than entertainment; less hostile contemporary commentary suggests an audience composed of the middle-class intelligentsia. Granville Barker's original concept for a season at the Court proposed a maximum price of admission of five or six shillings; in the event the prices were Stalls, 10s. 6d., Balcony Stalls, 7s. 6d., Upper Circle, 5s. and 4s., Pit, 2s. 6d., Gallery, 1s. Whatever its intellectual and ideological leanings, the constitution of the Court's audience derived from an identical socio-economic grouping to that of the major commercial theatres. Notwithstanding the frequent satirical jibes at the nature of the spectators, press reports of several Court productions describe audiences containing the fashionable and the famous. When the topical political satire of Shaw's *John Bull's Other Island*, first staged at the Court in 1904, could be enjoyed by Campbell-Bannerman, Asquith, and Balfour (he saw the play several times) it is difficult to envisage precisely who was being offended.

Nevertheless, the nature of much minority drama must have made the experience of visiting the theatre a different thing from watching Jones's *Mrs Dane's Defence* or Pinero's *His House in Order*. Other aspects of the theatrical experience, however, were not so easily modified. In 1913 Barker was in management with his wife Lillah McCarthy at the St James's. There is some irony in the fact that, in the very theatre where George Alexander had shone as the *raisonneur* in Pinero's plays, a notice stated 'we should like our patrons to feel that in no part of the house is evening dress indispensable'. But the graduated pricing policy at the Court, and similarly at other ventures including the St James's, carried the same implications as it did for the commercial theatre. A cartoon 'Shavians at the Savoy', which appeared in the *Bystander* of 2 October 1907 (reproduced in both Kennedy and Holroyd) presents Shaw in messianic pose hectoring the assembled masses. Despite its satirical insinuations, the cartoon's depiction of a Shavian audience shows precisely those sartorial demarcations associated with the various parts of the house fulsomely described by Macqueen-Pope. Some aspects of theatre-going as social activity are not to be changed merely by a change in the bill of fare. A problem was that, whatever the nature of the minority drama, it was staged in theatres which both previously and later housed the commercial drama. And the social and ideological values of the commercial stage were inscribed in the theatre buildings themselves. The minority theatre, like the commercial theatre, was not without its contradictions.

The achievement of the various minority theatre ventures was considerable. It effected a change in the climate of theatrical opinion and indicated the possibility of a different theatrical organization which could promote different sorts of drama. The consequences of both its experiments and achievements are central to the development of twentieth-century theatre. Yet, within the late Victorian and Edwardian period itself, it brought about little real change in the structural or institutional hegemony of the theatre.

Statistical postscript

Histories and surveys of late Victorian and Edwardian drama and theatre often create the impression that Jones and Pinero were to all intents and purposes spent forces by the start of the twentieth century and the running was with the 'new' dramatists Galsworthy, Granville Barker and Shaw. The figures below, extrapolated from J. P. Wearing's *The London Stage 1890–1919*, demonstrate the actual presence on the London stage of the dramatists discussed in this book. Table 1 gives the total number of performances for each dramatist throughout the period.

TABLE 1

	1890–9	1900–9	1910–19	Total
Jones	2056	1147	487	3690
Pinero	2478	1278	1078	4834
Galsworthy	—	60	230	290
Barker	15	87	129	231
Shaw	78	1008	1482	2568

As one can see the presence of the plays by Galsworthy and Barker in the theatre was minimal in comparison to the other three. Jones and Pinero admittedly were at their most prominent during the 1890s, but Pinero maintained a very effective presence throughout the next two decades and Jones only markedly dropped off in the third. What distinguishes Shaw from either Galsworthy or Barker is that his presence in the second and third decades matches that of the commercial dramatists.

Table 2 gives the average run of each individual production for Jones, Pinero and Shaw.

TABLE 2

	1890–9	1900–9	1910–19
Jones	64	67	54
Pinero	83	67	63
Shaw	26	28	71

Shaw's are the figures to note. Although the total number of performances of his plays in the second and third decades matches that of Jones and Pinero, the average run between 1900 and 1909 indicates the effect of his promotion by the repertory and short-run systems of the minority theatre. In the third decade Shaw's profile is much more like that of a commercial dramatist; both productions of new plays and revivals of plays initially staged by the minority theatre are achieving long runs and becoming an acceptable proposition for commercial managements.

Table 2 should be set against Table 3 which gives the average run of the first production of plays by Jones and Pinero.

TABLE 3

	1890–9	1900–9	1910–19
Jones	120	86	67
Pinero	126	142	78

Jones's new work shows a steady decline as the period progresses. Pinero, however, is at his strongest during the second decade and fades significantly in the third. The equivalent figure for Shaw in the third decade is 99. This includes three minor one-act pieces – *The Dark Lady of the Sonnets* (1910), *The Music Cure* (1914) and *The Inca of Perusalem* (1917) – which received only one performance each. If these are excluded from the statistics the average run becomes 147 and clearly matches that of successful commercial dramatists.

11
Jones and Pinero

Neither Henry Arthur Jones nor Arthur Wing Pinero started their careers in the theatre or came from theatrical families. Jones was born in 1851 at Grandesborough, Buckinghamshire, into a family of tenant farmers. Leaving school at the age of twelve, he worked as a draper's assistant in Ramsgate and Gravesend before moving to London in 1869. Between 1870 and 1879 he worked as a commercial traveller for drapery firms in London, Bradford, and Exeter. In 1879 he gave up his employment in trade to devote himself entirely to playwriting. Pinero was born into a family of Portuguese origin in 1855. Both his father and grandfather were members of the legal profession. At the age of ten he began to take some part in his father's work and between 1870 and 1874 he was engaged as a solicitor's clerk in Lincoln's Inn Fields. In 1884 he became a full-time professional playwright. The early careers of neither man pointed to the stage and their entry into the theatre took different paths.

Jones's upbringing in lower-middle-class, provincial, non-conformist circles, where, he recalls, 'dancing, card-playing and theatre going were vices' (Cordell, p. 21), was not conducive to his later career. Despite the curtailment of his formal education and the demands of his employment, Jones embarked upon a rigorous process of self-education:

> I never had a day's schooling afterwards [i.e. starting work], and I consider this to have been a great advantage. I was able to educate myself in my own way and at my own expense, by keeping up a constant and loving acquaintance with the English classics, and with some of the French and German master-pieces; by a close study of social and political economy; and by extensive foragings among the sciences. (D. A. Jones, p. 31).

Jones's reading in nineteenth-century non-fictional prose (notably Huxley and Spencer) was to have a profound influence on the construction of character and plot in his dramatic writing. But the more important schooling came from the professional theatre itself. Jones visited the theatre for the first time after his arrival in London; the experience was to change the course of his life. He abandoned previous attempts to write fiction in favour of drama and devoted his leisure time to seeing plays. He applied the same diligence and earnestness to his new-found interest as he had to his previous self-education: 'I used to hurry from the City almost every evening at six to see the same successful play for perhaps a dozen times, till I could take its mechanism to pieces' (D. A. Jones, p. 34). For Jones the essential problem was one of a play's construction. Much nineteenth-century drama depended upon formulas of mechanical and contrived plotting. Jones's analyses of these mechanisms, coupled with the mechanistic bent of his other intellectual inquiries, places him firmly in the temper of his age both within the theatre and without. From 1870 onwards he effectively taught himself to write plays in his spare time using as his tutor the available offerings of the professional Victorian stage.

Pinero was also a keen playgoer but unlike Jones the substance of his early experience of professional theatre was gained from actually working in it. Concurrent with his employment as a solicitor's clerk, Pinero enrolled as a member of the Elocution Class of Birkbeck Literary and Scientific Institution (now Birkbeck College). The class regularly mounted plays and recitals in the College theatre and even undertook a tour of the provinces. In 1874 Pinero took leave of both the legal profession and the amateur stage and embarked upon a career as a professional actor. He secured positions in provincial stock companies in Edinburgh and Liverpool where he had the opportunity to act with visiting stars such as E. A. Sothern, Mrs Scott-Siddons, and Charles Mathews. These performers had established their reputations earlier in the century but continued to undertake provincial tours in which they would take the leading role supported by the members of the resident stock company. In 1876 he returned to London to join Irving's company at the Lyceum, and in 1881 he was engaged by the Bancrofts at the Haymarket until his retirement from performance in 1884. During his ten years' professional work on the stage, Pinero gained valuable experience in the provinces and played in two of the foremost companies in London. Most importantly for his future career, he acquired a thorough knowledge of the requirements and scope of the contemporary professional theatre and its drama. Whilst continuing his acting career in London, Pinero began to turn his hand to acquiring the techniques of writing plays.

Their routes were different but one fact is crucial for both men. They were both schooled by a thorough observation of, amongst other modes of dramatic writing, nineteenth-century models of farce, sentimental comedy, and domestic melodrama. In their early work, one-act curtain-raisers, both writers not only drew heavily on the plot structures and character types of these models, but showed a more fundamental affiliation to the emotional structures, ethical intonation, and moral definition of such drama. If they had stopped writing at this point, their work would merely exist amongst the thousands of other items which make up the handlists of plays in Allardyce Nicoll's *A History of the English Drama*. Pinero, however, went on to make his mark with a series of farces, *The Magistrate* (1885), *The Schoolmistress* (1886), and *Dandy Dick* (1887), and Jones's first notable play was his melodrama *The Silver King* (1882). All these works demonstrate the authors' mastery of the conventions and formulas of farce and domestic melodrama. Although they are generally perceived to be superior to many other nineteenth-century offerings in similar genres, it is probably only with the benefit of hindsight that one can detect in their work of the 1880s features which would make Jones and Pinero the foremost dramatists of the next decade. What should not be ignored is how well they had learnt their lessons. The significance of their mastery of established convention and formula is that, particularly in the case of Jones, the habits they had learnt in their apprenticeship remained with them. Despite the efforts they made to extend the range and tone of the drama, their work throughout their careers tended to exhibit a more sophisticated and refined version of those habits.

Jones was a tireless pamphleteer, essay and letter writer on behalf of the drama. He reiterated the same handful of maxims throughout his career with a constant aim: 'to gain for myself and to spread amongst playgoers a knowledge of those facts and conditions and rules which will help to develop an intellectual drama in England, and to make our theatre an object of national pride and esteem' (H. A. Jones, 1913, p. vii). His firm belief was that the drama was capable of expressing an intellectual rigour which would stand the test of being placed alongside the best thought and literature of the day. Although Pinero did not try to match Jones as a polemicist, his beliefs were similar. Once their careers had been established, they were, in their society drama of the 1890s, poised to put their beliefs into practice.

Their society drama, in its mediation of upper-middle-class life, goes beyond a descriptive presentation of the modes of behaviour and codes of conduct of that class, to a more fundamental allegiance to the ideological underpinning of such mores. Domestic melodrama throughout the nineteenth century was often blatantly populist in its appeal. The endorsed moral centre frequently resided in the oppressed, and the 'poor but honest' working class. As a result of the way in which the melodrama mediates structures of power, class, and wealth, those with money and of superior social class were frequently presented in the roles of wicked seducers, stony-hearted foreclosing landlords, and the like. Jones's full-length plays of the 1880s, *The Silver King*, *Saints and Sinners* (1884), *The Middleman* (1889), for example, all draw for their intonation and definition from this tradition. But the shifting, in class terms, of the central dramatic focus of the society drama also shifts the ideological centres of the plays so that the endorsed ideological constructs are those of the dominant class.

Both Jones and Pinero advocated the desirability, and even the necessity, of the drama's compliance with the social and political orthodoxies of the day. A reiterated maxim of Jones is that 'The wise statesman does not attempt to make laws too far in advance of the moral and intellectual condition of the people. Nor does the wise playwright forget that playwriting is very rigorously limited in similar respects' (H. A. Jones, 1895, pp. 99–100). Any sense that this constitutes a serious limitation was one that Jones was perfectly willing to observe in his own practice. 'I would not,' he claimed, 'willingly offend any single person among my audience; indeed I would, at some violence to my own convictions, remove any scene that would hurt the natural reverence of any spectator' (H. A. Jones, 1895, p. 50). Pinero held a similar belief in the functional relationship between the drama and the dominant ideology: 'I assert unhesitatingly that the instinct by which the public feels that one form of drama, and not another, is what best satisfies its intellectual and spiritual needs at this period or at that is a natural and justified instinct' (Pinero, p. 65). Pinero, as a dramatist working in the commercial theatre, understood and asserted the congruity between the social and cultural nexus of both consumers and providers of popular drama. Whilst he recognized that 'the intellectual and spiritual needs' were only relative to the age, the overriding implication of the positions both dramatists took is that the ideological formations they acknowledged were natural and therefore inevitable, sacrosanct and, ultimately, unquestionable. Deviance from them would be at best perverse and probably against the essence of human nature. For Jones in particular, these formations constituted eternal and permanent values which it was the function of the theatre to exhibit. Despite the inevitable discrepancies and contradictions between practice and theory, the tendency of the ideological positions of Jones and Pinero results in a drama which is not just reflective or expressive of the ideology of the dominant class. The drama is deliberately organized, in its formal construction and systems of ethical validation, so as to be instrumental in endorsing orthodox ideological assumptions. Furthermore, Pinero realized, its effectiveness depended upon a mediation of an idealized version of contemporary orthodoxies: 'I believe . . . that the playwright's finest task is that of giving back to the multitude their own thoughts and conceptions illuminated, enlarged, and, if needful, purged, perfected, transfigured' (Kobbé, p. 128). The playwright must construct society rather than reflect it. The issue of whether what happens in society drama is realistic, in the sense of a matter-of-fact depiction of what actually happens in upper-middle-class society, must be a secondary consideration or possibly even immaterial. It is not accurate reflection but an active endorsement of dominant ideological constructs which is the primary ordering principle of the drama.

A problem both dramatists shared was how to avoid the offence which Ibsen's critique of society provoked and still provide a drama which appeared to be equally searching, serious and sophisticated in its treatment of contemporary social issues. The peculiar tone of society drama derives from the tensions within a kind of play which, whilst it is ultimately supportive rather than challenging of society's values, aims at a thorough-going examination of those values. The central issue, to aspects of which Jones and Pinero returned repeatedly, focuses on the implications and effects of deviance from the codes and structures by which upper-middle-class society defines and regulates relations between the sexes.

Jones's *Mrs Dane's Defence* (1900) exhibits many of the features and strategies of society drama. At the start of the play the captivating Mrs Dane is turning the heads of most of the men and, in particular, that of Lionel Carteret, a young man of twenty-four, who has fallen extravagantly in love with her. In doing so he jilts Janet Colquhoun to whom he is unofficially engaged. Sir Daniel, a high-court judge by profession and Lionel's adoptive father, is opposed to the attachment between Lionel and Mrs Dane. The opposition, initially founded partly on his sense of the immaturity and folly of Lionel's attachment and partly on the fact that nothing is known of Mrs Dane's background, is intensified when a rumour circulates that she is allegedly a Felicia Hindemarsh who was involved in a scandal in Vienna some four years previously. Hindemarsh, then employed as a governess, had an affair with her employer and it is later revealed that a child resulted from the relationship. Even though the initial allegation has been withdrawn, the flames of the scandal are fanned by a Mrs Bulsom-Porter, an objectionable and persistent scandalmonger, who makes it her life's work to sniff out and expose those who have erred. Society's rules are inexorable. If the story is true then Mrs Dane is rendered not only totally unfit to be Lionel's wife but also to be a member of society as it is constituted in the play. The mere suggestion that there may be some cloud in her past is sufficient for her to be immediately snubbed and ostracized. Sir Daniel is implacable in his support of society's regulations regarding Mrs Dane. Nevertheless, he relents towards her and is prepared to condone the match only if her innocence, that she is Mrs Dane and not Felicia Hindemarsh, can be proved. Mrs Dane sets about providing the evidence and he undertakes her defence by collating and testing the evidence to refute Mrs Bulsom-Porter's continuing slurs. All seems to be going well until, in the third act, a chance discovery in a topographical dictionary alerts him to inconsistencies in her story and after a climactic cross-examination scene, in which he draws upon his courtroom experience, he confronts her with the momentous words, 'Woman, you're lying!'. Mrs Dane is Felicia Hindemarsh.

Although the main issue of the play, the exposure of Mrs Dane, has been resolved, the final act is crucial to the intonation of society drama. Five people other than Mrs Dane know the truth: Risby, who knew of Hindemarsh in Vienna, a private detective engaged by Mrs Bulsom-Porter, Lionel, Lady Eastney and Sir Daniel. Risby and the detective agree to say nothing, similarly Lionel will not injure the women he loves. Sir Daniel and Lady Eastney say nothing so that a comic humiliation can be inflicted upon Mrs Bulsom-Porter. She is forced to present a written apology to Mrs Dane which causes the scandalmonger something approaching a mental and physical collapse.

Lionel, however, in defiance of society's edicts, is still in the grip of his romantic infatuation and determined to marry Mrs Dane. Sir Daniel persuades her that if she acquiesces in Lionel's impetuousness she will only make him unhappy and she vows to give him up. As Mrs Dane is not to be publicly exposed, there is a sense in which she can still exist in society. In response to her question as to whether Lady Eastney will continue to receive her, Lady Eastney, after a significant moment of hesitation, agrees to be 'at home' if Mrs Dane should call. But, as Mrs Dane takes her leave, the last words she utters in the play create a different impression; they are founded on an image of exclusion from society as defined by the play: 'Now, Sir Daniel, you shall see me outside the palings – no further. I shall see my boy to-morrow' (Act 4). Further, she acknowledges, by the reference to her son, her own sense of accountability for her past conduct. It is difficult to envisage that Lady Eastney will find herself in the awkward position of having to be at home to Mrs Dane.

Of course, the other people who know the truth about Mrs Dane are the audience. What they have experienced is a demonstration that her sort of behaviour cannot pay off, and that the potential disturbance represented by her attempt to re-enter society by marrying Lionel has been successfully parried and will count for nothing. At the end of the play it is intimated that Lionel will almost certainly marry Janet as he should have done in the first place. The only other issue to be resolved in the last act is effected when Lady Eastney consents to become the wife of Sir Daniel.

The figure of the woman with a past is a commonplace of Victorian fiction. In the drama the figure descends from the vogue for wicked ladies of earlier melodrama, and the ethical structuring which defined, for instance, the eponymous villainess of *Lady Audley's Secret* (1863) would continue to determine, albeit with more sophisticated modulations, the dramatic possibilities of the figure when she, and the threat she was perceived to represent to the fabric of society, became a frequent feature of society drama. The woman with a past was titillating and exciting but safely and reassuringly contained by a dramatic action which imposed appropriate punishments for unorthodox behaviour. Pinero's *The Second Mrs Tanqueray* (1893), whilst appearing to do something different, is symptomatic.

The first act shows Aubrey Tanqueray in his bachelor chambers giving a supper party to three long-established men friends. One of them, Cayley Drummle, arrives late. He has been consoling Lady Orreyed as her son has compacted a marriage to someone whose past should disqualify her from society. He pronounces society's verdict: 'You may dive into many waters, but there is *one* social Dead Sea.' Drummle is unwittingly tactless, for the supper party has been called so that Tanqueray, impeccably respectable, can impart the information that he is about to marry similarly. His wife-to-be, Paula, has previously had numerous liaisons in the *demi-monde* of Europe. Tanqueray acknowledges society's strictures, for the party is by way of a farewell to his friends. He will accept the ensuing ostracism and retire to his country house with his wife where they will live as solitary pariahs. The first act serves a function beyond exposition. Two of Tanqueray's friends disappear from the drama altogether; their absence is the embodiment of the social edict. It is only the fact that Drummle is a bachelor, and therefore has a greater latitude, which allows him to continue his friendship. The rest of the play examines the failure of the marriage.

Paula's first appearance in the play, after Tanqueray's guests have left, demonstrates a series of social solecisms. Pinero's strategy accords with a convention of nineteenth-century drama which uses initial signifiers to place characters firmly within a system of ethical definition whose edicts will usually be fulfilled by the action of the play. But it seems as if Pinero is to go beyond this and utilize the theoretically more neutral formal conventions of literary naturalism to explain Paula's character and subsequent events in her career. She is presented as being a victim of society. In the first act, Aubrey unequivocally propounds a critique of those formations, enshrined in a male hegemony, which both create and condemn the position into which women like Paula are forced as an act of survival. In the second act, however, it is insinuated that her behaviour patterns result predominantly from the moral implications of her previous dissolute experience. Her husband describes her:

There's hardly a subject you can broach on which poor Paula hasn't some strange, out-of-the-way thought to give utterance to; some curious, warped notion. They are not mere worldly thoughts – unless, good God! they belong to the little hellish world which our blackguardism has created: no, her ideas have too little calculation in them to be called worldly. But it makes it the more dreadful that such thoughts should be ready, spontaneous; that expressing them has become a perfectly natural process; that her words, acts even, have almost lost their proper significance for her, and seem beyond her control. Ah, and the pain of listening to it all from the woman one loves, the woman one hoped to make happy and contented, who is really and truly a good woman, as it were, maimed! (Act 2)

Aubrey's assumption here of a more orthodox position and its vocabulary is borne out by what the audience sees of her behaviour. Pinero shows she is fit neither for society nor the position of his wife. What is crucial is that her behaviour, whatever its cause, is defined purely by its deviance from a standard determined by the dominant code. Aubrey's speech articulates tensions between competing systems of causation and judgemental definition – critique of society, endorsement of society's codes of behaviour, and a relationship between society's codes and a larger ethical system – which inform the play as a whole.

The contradictions in Aubrey derive, of course, from the habits of a man of his class and background, but they result more specifically from a twist in the plot introduced by Pinero. Ellean, his daughter from his first marriage, returns unexpectedly to her father's home after a long estrangement. He is now forced to acknowledge that the idea of a successful self-imposed quarantine, upon which his marriage was to be based, is not possible. Moreover, he accepts as valid society's view that a woman with a past is a contamination when it is his daughter who is exposed to it. The crux of the issue is that Paula is unfit to be stepmother to his daughter.

Ellean, like Paula, is initially defined by a set of determinants deriving from the conventions of literary naturalism. Her disposition is an inheritance from her frigid Roman Catholic mother compounded by the experience of her upbringing in an Irish convent. She is rendered unfit for normal society life by an uncompromisingly unworldly, unemotional religiosity. Her inaptitude, however, is social rather than moral. It is in Pinero's subsequent treatment of these two characters that it becomes implicit that the naturalistic definition is underpinned by certain ethical assumptions. Ellean, under the guidance of the kindly and sociable Mrs Cortelyon, is taken to Paris where, in a matter of weeks, she is able to cast off both inheritance and conditioning and learn to live and love in accordance with the accepted modes of behaviour of her peers. Paula has initially had a childhood as innocent and pure as Ellean's. Aubrey tells her: 'I know what you were at Ellean's age. I'll tell you. You hadn't a thought that wasn't a wholesome one, you hadn't an impulse that didn't tend towards good, you never harboured a notion you couldn't have gossiped about to a parcel of children' (Act 3). But once she has deviated from the code which governs sexual conduct, the change in her behaviour is irrevocable. Unlike Ellean, who is able to escape her determinants because of a new environment, Paula, even when removed from her previous life, has slipped beyond redemption.

At this point, the precise relationship between the naturalistic conception of character and the promotion of what is substantially a set of ethical judgements is uneasy and ambiguous. It is only in the events after Ellean's return from Paris that the primary principle of definition makes itself fully apparent. When she returns, she is accompanied by Ardale, an apparently eligible suitor. In the first act, before Paula marries Aubrey, she hands him a letter containing details of her past liaisons; Aubrey, as a gesture of generosity, burns the letter without reading it. Ardale's name was included in the letter. The Tanquerary marriage finally ends in disaster. Paula commits suicide at the end of the play not because of the inevitability of the suggested naturalistic determinants but because of a contrivance in the plot whereby there occurs a coincidental meeting between Ardale and Ellean in Paris. The play is so constructed as to provide a resolution which actively endorses the validity of the dominant codes of behaviour and ethics. This then becomes the primary system of definition and subordinates, and even abrogates, other systems, such as literary naturalism, mooted earlier in the play.

The technique derives in part from French models of the well-made play as practised by Scribe through to Sardou and adapted to English usage. There is another more indigenous precursor in nineteenth-century British melodrama where the plot structure creates its own universe which upholds melodrama's ethical assumptions. The coincidence of Ardale's and Ellean's meeting in Paris, as with the seemingly accidental discovery of the truth about Mrs Dane, point to the fact, as perceived by Pinero and Jones, that attempts of women with pasts to re-enter society are fated to fail. Clayton Hamilton, Pinero's editor, responded to more than a theatrical expectation implicit in the burning of Paula's letter: 'We feel instinctively that the ghost of some experience recorded in that letter will rise up subsequently, to curse both Paula and himself. This feeling is so emphatic that it afflicts us almost with the force of that *nemesis* which was customarily foreshadowed by the tragic dramatists of ancient Greece' (*Social Plays of A. W. Pinero*, I, p.42). For him the plotting of the play offered evidence of a universal retributive justice. The aesthetic of the well-made play is in essence a function of the endorsement of the dominant ideology for the plays are structured so that transgressions against the dominant code eventually will out and those who, according to that code, deserve stricture, will be dealt with appropriately.

One of the things deemed appropriate in the distribution of rewards and punishments in Jones's *The Dancing Girl* (1891) is an emphatic endorsement of the double standard of morality. Drusilla Ives, seduced by the Duke of Guisebury, disappears from the play at the end of the third act and, the audience is later informed, dies after dancing in public in New Orleans on a Sunday night. The Duke, on the other hand, is able to make reparation through good works. The dramatic centre of the final act lies in his reformation and rehabilitation within the very community from which he seduced Drusilla. At the height of its sophistication the society drama would rarely have recourse to a plot structure which so crudely endorsed the double standard. Yet in *The Second Mrs Tanqueray*, despite Aubrey's attack on the double standard, Pinero does not feel obliged to make Ardale emulate Paula and commit suicide. Ardale's punishment is to be ostracized from the immediate Tanqueray circle but not, like Mrs Dane, from the whole of society.

Jones's *The Case of Rebellious Susan* (1894) concerns itself with whether Lady Susan Harabin can repay her husband's adultery in its own kind. In comparison to the challenging note of Tanqueray's indictment of the double standard, Jones's play is far more at ease with its initial premise about male and female sexual misconduct: 'What is sauce for the goose will never be sauce for the gander. In fact, there is no gander sauce' (Act 1). James Harabin is admonished for his persistent and flagrant lapses, but there is never any suggestion that he should therefore forfeit his position in society as would be the case had Susan Harabin so behaved. Such features should hardly need further exemplification or elaboration for a modern audience or reader. The whole of society drama is suffused with the double morality and its attendant sexism, but not, as it purports, because it accurately reflects contemporary upper-middle-class society. The society drama needs the double standard for a kingpin in its endorsement of what is a more extensive conservative ideology and sexual politics. The functional importance of the figure of the woman with a past is that society is defined as much by those who are excluded as those who are approbated.

The deep-rooted structural sexism of society drama manifests itself, beyond its endorsement of the double standard, in constructions of gender which accord with dominant and traditionalist views. In 1884, Jones adapted *A Doll's House* under the title *Breaking a Butterfly*, a notorious effort which later caused him some embarrassment. Nora, transmuted into the figure of Flora – familiarly Flossie – Goddard, instead of asserting unfeminine independence and self-determination by slamming the door and walking out of her doll's house, chooses to remain in the sheltered safety of her husband's home and protection. In doing so she earns her husband's commendation – 'Flossie was a child yesterday: to-day she is a woman' (Act 3). *Breaking a Butterfly* owes more to domestic melodrama than it does to Ibsen in more than just Flora's affirmation of a conventional nineteenth-century ideal of wifely submission and duty. But a version of that ideal, seemingly far more sophisticatedly treated when presented as a more fraught and precarious concept, remains as an ideal construct of femininity and a pattern of appropriate behaviour in the society drama.

Pinero's *His House in Order* (1906) uses the construct quite patently as a device of judgemental definition. Nina, the second wife of Filmer Jesson, is initially presented as insouciant and irresponsible in all practical matters, and thus compares extremely unfavourably with the first Mrs Jesson, apparently a model of domestic order and rectitude. The vulgar and narrow-minded relatives of the first wife continually humiliate Nina by constant reference and comparison to the predecessor. However, a trick of chance places in Nina's hands evidence that the woman she is humbled before had been an adultress. Much of the subsequent dramatic action is taken up with the question of whether the second Mrs Jesson will take her revenge on those who have slighted her by exposing the first. A girl/woman opposition, similar to that of *Breaking a Butterfly*, is invoked. Nina perceives herself moving from girlhood to womanhood when she attains and intends to use the power the incriminating letters give her. But true womanhood, the play proposes, resides not in defiance and independence by using the evidence but in Nina's decision, partly brought about by an acceptance of the persuasive reasoning and advice of Filmer's more genial brother Hilary, that she should assume the mantle of acquiescence and self-sacrifice of the dutiful wife.

The judicial system of the play demands that Filmer learn the truth about his first wife and recognize the true worth of his second, that the vulgar relatives should be discomfited, and that Maurewarde, the first wife's lover, should, like Ardale, be expelled from the immediate circle. The performance of these tasks, unfit for a woman, falls to Hilary. *His House in Order* fully endorses this construct of appropriate female behaviour, and Nina, throughout the whole of the play, is defined and ultimately vindicated by her relationship to the construct. The consonance between the ideological assumptions of play and playgoers may be assumed from the fact *His House in Order* enjoyed the longest run of any play by Pinero during the period.

The key intonation for women is renunciation, and its centrality as a definer of female behaviour accounts for the complexity of tone at the endings of Jones's *The Case of Rebellious Susan* and *The Liars* (1897). Lady Susan and Lady Jessica, after being on the point of breaking out, grudgingly return to what are patently less than perfect marriages, but, at the same time, their submission to dominant social formations and male authority is approbated by the cardinal defining assumptions of the society drama. The intonation is also crucial to the depiction of women who have irreparably blotted their moral copy books. Both Mrs Dane and Mrs Ebbsmith, in Pinero's *The Notorious Mrs Ebbsmith* (1895), choose at some cost to themselves to relinquish the men whose futures they threaten. Their renunciation, like that of Isabel Vine in the numerous stage adaptations of *East Lynne*, enables them to regain, despite their moral standing, the presumed sympathy and respect of their audiences. It is, however, a sign of the greater urbanity and sophistication of society drama that, whereas Isabel Vine's final reparation and punishment lie in death, Mrs Dane's and Mrs Ebbsmith's lie in behaviour compliant with those very codes which condemn them and demand their ostracism. They effect their own expulsion and thus there is a further endorsement of society's codes when the good sense of such codes is acknowledged even by those who fall victim to them.

Central to the ideological structure of renunciation is the concept of duty. The construct of masculinity is not exempt from those intonations which define female behaviour. David Remon, in Jones's *The Masqueraders* (1894), preserves a conventional Victorian image of idealized womanhood and the ideology of domesticity when he renounces what he sees as his only chance of real happiness:

DAVID: . . . I love her! I love her! I love her! You shan't reason me out of my happiness!

HELEN: (*Stopping him*) I can't reason at all. I can only feel, and I know my instinct is right. I know the woman who gives herself to another man while her husband is alive betrays her sex, and is a bad woman.

DAVID: I love her! I love her! (*Going towards door*).

HELEN: (*Stopping him*) Then make your love the best thing in her life, and the best thing in yours. You have loved her so well. You have made so many sacrifices for her. Make this one last sacrifice. Keep her pure for her child. (Act 4)

The absolutist ethic and melodramatic intonation also informs Pinero's *The Profligate* (1891) where the suicide of the protagonist Dunstan Renshaw, prefiguring Paula Tanqueray's, constitutes an ultimate renunciation and atonement.

Both Remon and Renshaw shoulder, in different ways, the burden of maintaining the ideal of the institution of marriage. But the concept of male duty is predominantly a more pragmatic and mundane affair, public rather than domestic. In *The Notorious Mrs Ebbsmith*, the real threat represented by Agnes Ebbsmith's *de facto* marriage to Lucas Cleeve is that it will ruin his promising political career. This is so central to the structuring of the play that the efforts of Cleeve's family to prise him from the relationship are made so as to restore him not to legal wife but to career. His intention to co-write with Agnes Ebbsmith feminist tracts denouncing the institution of marriage is discountenanced as mere folly. Appropriate male roles can only be constituted in orthodox formations of public service. This proposition is more explicitly founded in an image of late Victorian and Edwardian Britain as an imperial and military power. The imagery which defines David Remon's moment of temptation is of military betrayal, desertion and cowardice. Remon's duty is to conduct an astronomical survey in Africa; *The Liars* presents a more specific form of colonial duty. Edward Falkner's intention to dally illicitly with Jessica Nepean in England will prevent him from returning to Africa where, we are told, he is the only man who can deal with the native chiefs and so save thousands of lives. The epitaph which is predicted for him if he follows this course of action is explicit in its assumption of the attributes by which male conduct is judged: 'Sold his honour, his fame, his country, his duty, his conscience, his all, for a petticoat!' (Act 4). Falkner, like other young men in his situation, gives up his love to do his duty in the essentially male domain of the colonies. This constitutes a form of atonement for past indiscretion and promises a means of forgetting unfortunate emotional entanglements. Renunciation of one's heart's desire means something very different for men than for women. For women the act of renunciation is offered as an end in itself and it thus subscribes to dominant gender attributes of passivity and submission; for men renunciation is a sacrifice, but one which enables their integration into public structures of social and institutional activity.

In this respect, just as women with pasts compromise the institution of marriage, it is women in general who are represented as an intrusion and disturbance which actively endangers the construct of male duty. Despite the centrality that this would seem to afford to women in the dramatic action of the plays, the primacy of this construction of female role and identity within the drama renders women, in relation to the male world, essentially unimportant and trivial. This is the sort of view of women which forms the advice which puts Falkner back on the right track:

> Love 'em, worship 'em, make the most of 'em! Go down on your knees every day and thank God for having sent them into this dreary world for our good and comfort. But, don't break your heart over 'em! Don't ruin your career for 'em! Don't lose a night's rest for 'em! They aren't worth it . . . ! (Act 3)

A further consequence is that women are not allowed social positions on their own account but only in relation to men. Thus women in the society drama are ranged around a variety of options with marriage at their centre; those acceptable to society are wife, widow, and eligible spinster. Even within these categories the primary definition for women is moral rather than social. Thus, the disquisition on a wife's duty in *The Masqueraders* indicates the constitution of female civic and social obligation only in relation to male authority and dominant moral structures. Her duty is 'to her husband to keep her vows. To herself to keep herself pure and stainless, because it is her glory . . . To society, to her nation, because no nation has ever survived whose women have been immoral' (Act 3). For women like Mrs Tanqueray, Mrs Ebbsmith, and Mrs Dane, whose past behaviour denies them access to socially approbated categories, the *only* possible definition is ultimately dependent upon their moral status.

What is also implicitly proposed is a notion of natural femininity which must find expression via conventionally approbated formations of sexual relations; the underlying implication is overtly stated in *The Case of Rebellious Susan*: 'There is an immense future for women as wives and mothers, and a very limited future for them in any other capacity . . . Nature's darling woman is a stay-at-home woman, a woman who wants to be a good wife and a good mother, and cares very little for anything else' (Act 3). Marriage then becomes the only truly safe position for women, hence the desire of Mrs Dane *et al* to be reinstated and the ultimate refusal of Susan Harabin and other married women to break out. The effect of society drama as a whole is not, as Jones believed of *The Case of Rebellious Susan*, to explore critically the socialization of women. It is to approve it.

This patterning of society drama can hardly accommodate a mediation of the experience of women independent of the structures of male authority. Pinero's *Iris* (1901) is indicative of how the drama shirks the presentation of female independence. Iris, a wealthy widow of twenty-six, is impoverished by the fraudulent activity of the solicitor who manages her investments. This development of the plot provides no real examination of her social and economic position but is introduced primarily to render her vulnerable to the theatrically more familiar machinations of a seducer figure. Her inability to cope with straitened circumstances is similarly mediated not as her interaction with socio-economic forces prejudicial to a woman alone in society, but as a failure of strength of will and character, an offence against the moral imperative of self-help. Her defeat has therefore an essentially moral implication.

Even more difficult for the society drama to accommodate seriously is the woman who proposes an independence founded upon an ideological position which openly conflicts with its fundamental assumptions and constructions of gender. The figures of the New Woman and the suffragette become, in *The Case of Rebellious Susan*, Jones's *Judah* (1890), and Pinero's pointedly titled *The Weaker Sex* (1889), butts of comedy and victims of satirical attack. The plays suggest that the validity of feminist views can be dispensed with by visiting comic humiliation upon the heads of any offenders against the conventional codes or by engineering the eventual re-assertion of 'natural' femininity, which has been only temporarily submerged. Even *The Notorious Mrs Ebbsmith*, which Pinero conceived of as a fair and frank treatment of contemporary feminist thought, is, whilst a far more considerable play in this respect than *The Weaker Sex*, not immune from similar features. Pinero's representation of Agnes Ebbsmith is tinged with the anti-feminist satire and demonologizing travesty of the figure of the New Woman to be found in the popular press. She is thus defined more in terms of a decidedly masculinist vision of the New Woman than in relation to actual feminist belief or practice. This deflection is consolidated by Pinero's deft exchange of the first definition for further, theatrically more familiar typological definitions. At key points in the development of the action, Agnes Ebbsmith moves from being a New Woman to a brazen fallen woman, and finally to a penitent fallen woman. The strategy is crucial to the play's disproving of the validity of her feminism and its resolution which sees her convinced she is no radical thinker spearheading a movement of liberation but a wanton seductress who, knowing now the error of her ways, intends to retire to a life of religious penitence and prayer in the north of England.

What is remarkable about the society drama is that, whilst as a whole the concatenation of its strategies supports reactionary ideological constructs, the sophistication and skill with which they are implemented in individual plays mediates an experience seemingly far more liberal. The dramas establish at their onset complex social and moral problems: for instance, in *The Second Mrs Tanqueray*, 'Can a marriage between a *demi-mondaine* and a respectable upper-middle-class gentleman work?'; or, in *The Case of Rebellious Susan*, 'Can a woman openly repay her husband's adultery in its own kind and survive in society?'; or, in *The Notorious Mrs Ebbsmith*, 'Can a woman of socialist and feminist beliefs put them into practice by keeping house with a married man of some public importance?' Admittedly the answer to all these questions eventually turns out to be – 'No'. But it is the comforting safety of such conclusions that in itself allows the dramatists considerable latitude. Incidental cynicism and interim questioning, which might challenge the social and moral ortho-doxies and create the appearance of serious and provocative discussion of the issues, are permissible because they can be assimilated. This is also true of emotional responses. Sympathy can be afforded Mrs Tanqueray, Mrs Dane, Mrs Ebbsmith before, and even when, they are expelled from society precisely because they *are* so expelled. Similarly, the apparent cynicism of the ending of *The Case of Rebellious Susan*, where Susan, cir-cumscribed by society's options, returns to an unsatisfactory marriage bought off by what the Bond Street jewellers can offer and her wealthy husband afford, is subsumed by a sense of relief that not just social mores but the very fabric of society have been preserved.

The persistence with which things are not allowed to proceed as far as divorce flies in the face of the contemporary context. Divorce scandals in the 1890s were widely reported and avidly read. The dramatists' concern for making things right by the end of the plays was at one level a commercial consideration. But this in itself cannot obscure a further deep-rooted anxiety. The break-down of the codes which govern sexual relationships evoked fears of a wider and more far-reaching disintegration of social and political formations. Jones, in a defence of his own practice, identifies the extent of the deeper anxiety:

> I am still in favor of what is called bourgeois morality, because as a general rule a woman's departure from it is attended by much more disastrous consequences to the children than a man's departure . . . We have not yet had time to see the effects of our present code of sexual morality. Let us see how it works; let us watch its reactions upon the family – that is, upon the unit

of social structure . . . It is a physiological fact that throughout life a woman's brain and general anatomy is much nearer and more allied to a child's than a man's brain and anatomy . . . My incessant protest is not against knocking down faulty human institutions, but against the folly of banging one's head against the great first laws and principles upon which all human institutions, all civilization are founded; and also against the folly of treating such primary instincts as sex, religion, and patriotism as if they were opinions, instead of being, as they are, impulses and emotions which we cannot root out, but must guide and control as best we may. (Cordell, pp. 89–90)

Structurally central to Jones's and Pinero's manipulation of the strategies by which they engineered appropriate conclusions is the figure of the *raisonneur*. The *raisonneur* is granted an authority both by his position in the fictional world of the plays (the preponderance of minor artistocratic titles appended to the *raisonneurs* is not insignificant) and by the play's structural organization which centres the ideological burden of the drama on him. What he asserts is a knowledge of how society and people work. The supreme confidence with which he does this is vindicated because the action of the plays proves him to be right. Examples of the *raisonneur* figure include Drummle in *The Second Mrs Tanqueray*, Carteret in *Mrs Dane's Defence*, Hilary Jesson in *His House in Order*, Kato and Deering in *The Case of Rebellious Susan* and *The Liars*. The interventions of these characters in providing advice, comprising of models of appropriate response and behaviour and overt in its exposition of dominant social, moral, and gender orthodoxies, are crucial to the plot structures of the drama. The acceptance of such advice by, for instance, Nina Jesson, Susan Harabin, Jessica Nepean, and Mrs Dane, resolves issues in accordance with these orthodoxies. Indeed, Carteret's accidental discovery of Mrs Dane's past places him in the position of earthly surrogate of a universe dedicated to the preservation of the social and moral codes of the Edwardian upper-middle classes.

The institutional structure of the late Victorian and Edwardian theatre made the role of the *raisonneur* an ideal vehicle for the actor manager. Wyndham and Alexander excelled in the parts provided for them by Jones and Pinero. They could reinforce on stage the social image they created for themselves as managers of their theatres; and, in the figures they represented on stage, they could be seen to be instrumental in endorsing dominant ideological and moral codes which the acting profession had been traditionally perceived to offend.

The *raisonneur* figure is also crucial in its contribution to the sophisticated tone essential to the implementation of the strategies of society drama. The *raisonneur* may be confident and assertive, but he is rarely bullish. His pronouncements are unruffled, detached, controlled; his tone is pragmatic, slightly cynical, worldly-wise. As a man of the world he's seen it all before, and his frequent admission of his own youthful indiscretions merely lends credence to his claims to know what he's talking about. The counsel given to Edward Falkner and Jessica Nepean represents the tone at its most successful:

> Now! I've nothing to say in the abstract against running away with another man's wife! There may be planets where it is not only the highest ideal morality, but where it has the further advantage of being a practical way of carrying on society. But it has one fatal defect in our country today – it won't work! You know what we English are, Ned. We're not a bit better than our neighbours, but, thank God! we do pretend we are, and we do make it hot for anybody who disturbs that holy pretence. And take my word for it, my dear Lady Jessica, my dear Ned, it won't work. You know it's not an original experiment you're making. It has been tried before. Have you ever known it to be successful? (Act 4)

The indulgence in an apparently cynical defence of the hypocrisy of society's facades is a part of that sophistication which administered to the audiences mild shocks but no serious undermining of dominant orthodoxies. Above all, the *raisonneur*'s profession that his position is founded upon experience and knowledge rather than ideological, moral, or idealistic principle provides an incalculable benefit. The drama, but more specifically the *raisonneur*, can support and enforce conventional codes of behaviour, with all their ideological underpinnings, without any hint of being uncomfortably or unattractively idealistic or moralistic. For instance, Sir Daniel Carteret, by choosing not to expose Mrs Dane publically, can appear to be generous and compassionate especially when juxtaposed against the activity of the contemptible Mrs Bulsom-Porter. But his seemingly more genial methods effectively result in what is only a superficially less malicious version of precisely what she was working towards – the expulsion of Mrs Dane. The *raisonneur* role was thus doubly suited to the actor manager's image. Not only could he enforce conventional codes of conduct, but as he did so he could offer to his audience an urbanity and sophistication which were consonant with his star status. The extent of the contemporary subscription to the ideological and tonal strategies of the society drama is indicated by this description of Wyndham, the *raisonneur* of *The Liars*, *The Case of Rebellious Susan*, and *Mrs Dane's Defence*:

> He has a whimsical, half tender, wholly delightful way of scolding pretty women. He has all the time such a twinkle in his eye, such humorous curves around his lips, and there is so much *savoir faire* and experience at the back of his twinkle, so much belief in and regard for human nature in the smile. He always suggests such chivalry, such an almost old-fashioned courtesy and deference to women, that it is no wonder he is so popular with the sex, who while they demand women's rights, mounting platforms and rostrums, are always susceptible to those delicate attentions which are not woman's rights but her privileges. In depicting the cultured man of the world, too well bred to show any violent emotion, and with a surface veneer of cynicism, Charles Wyndham has no equal. He is suave, persuasive, tender by turns; he has all the good qualities of the English gentleman on the stage. (Shore, p. 39)

More than any individual actor manager's popularity, the success or failure of a whole play could depend upon the images embodied in his role.

The *raisonneur*'s domination is emblematic of the domination of male authority which is central to the ideological assumptions of society drama. Consequently, despite the frequency with which female characters grace the titles of such plays, women are only notionally central, and the notion that in apparently following Ibsen in *A Doll's House* and *Hedda Gabler* the plays seriously offered a critique of women's oppression in society is a sham. The ideological centre and the dramatic focus reside in male authority which in itself depends upon male constructs of appropriate female behaviour and sexuality. The last act of *Mrs Dane's Defence* exposes the sham. Lady Eastney makes a spirited attack on male hegemony and society's hypocrisy in its treatment of women, in response to which Sir Daniel becomes rather more heated than is customary. However, the function of the exchanges is not to present a real defence of Mrs Dane nor is Carteret's vociferousness an indication he's on the losing side. Their function is rather to provide Lady Eastney with an opportunity to offer herself in marriage and thus collude fully with male domination; with some amusement she closes the exchange: 'I rather like you in a temper. It shows me that if I marry you, you'd be my master' (Act 4). The actress Elizabeth Robins, prominent in early productions of Ibsen and author of the suffragette play *Votes for Women* (1907), remarked more acidly, 'What was wanted of women of the stage was, first and mainly, what was wanted outside – a knack of pleasing' (Hollege, p. 5).

Romances, such as that between Carteret and Lady Eastney, were fairly commonly provided for the actor manager and his leading lady. More than a sop to the actor manager's vanity, the romances have a function in the ideological structuring of the drama and are instrumental in overcoming what would otherwise be a tricky problem. That problem is how the dramatists were to maintain the concept of marriage as essential to society's fabric and to endorse female submission and obedience to male authority when the marriages presented are far from perfect and the husbands don't deserve to be obeyed. By a simple process of juxtaposition between the good sense with which the *raisonneur* conducts his relationship and the bad management of the marriages in, say, *The Liars* or *The Case of Rebellious Susan*, the actor manager and his leading lady could embody role models for the successful marriage. The proposition underlying the plays, that 'marriage is a perfect institution . . . worked by imperfect creatures' (*The Case of Rebellious Susan*, Act 1), could be proved true by the demonstration of positive and negative examples. The example of the *raisonneurs'* relationships indicates that marriage could successfully work in practice in spite of the difficulties presented by the Nepean or Harabin examples. The tone in which the *raisonneur's* relationship is conducted is commensurate with his overall deportment. His wooing is mature, rational, immune from effusive outbursts. In comparison to this role model of appropriate masculine behaviour, the emotional declarations of younger men like Lionel Carteret or Edward Falkner appear callow and ultimately silly. The implication of the plays is that the younger men will eventually realize this and emerge as potential *raisonneur* figures themselves. After all, the *raisonneurs* by their own admissions were often a little wayward in their youths.

The society drama's persistent concern with irregular relationships between the sexes is an indication of the suitability of this area of experience for a drama committed to the endorsement of dominant ideological codes. Deviations from the codes governing relationships between the sexes are depicted and accounted for as isolated romantic infatuations or sentimental aberrations on the part of certain individuals, and a critique of dominant codes or institutions is thus conveniently avoided. The tone of the *raisonneur*, congruous with the gentlemanly and genteel temper of the actor manager's theatre, averts any potential indelicacy and mediates this whole area of experience in socially inoffensive ways. Sex and sexuality become deodorized and laundered, subordinated, as Shaw noted, to an overriding emphasis on the social and judicial consequences of irregular relationships:

What is the usual formula for such plays? A woman has, on some past occasion, been brought into conflict with the law which regulates the relations of the sexes. A man, by falling in love with her, or marrying her, is brought into conflict with the social convention which discountenances the woman. Now the conflicts of individuals with law and convention can be dramatized like all other human conflicts; but they are purely judicial; and the fact that we are much more curious about the suppressed relations between the man and the woman than about the relations between both and our courts of law and private juries of matrons, produces that sensation of evasion, of dissatisfaction, of fundamental irrelevance, of shallowness, of useless disagreeableness, of total failure to edify and partial failure to interest, which is as familiar to you in the theatres as it was to me when I, too, frequented those uncomfortable buildings, and found our popular playwrights in the mind to (as they thought) emulate Ibsen. (*B H S*, II, pp. 496–7)

The suppression of the relationship between the man and the woman in favour of social and judicial conflicts is surely an essential function of the patterning of society drama. For if the relationship itself were to be investigated more deeply, the resultant shift in dramatic emphasis might suggest that the relationship had a seriousness, validity, and power which would threaten and so call into question the very ideological formations the society drama sought to endorse.

Jones's work, more than Pinero's, embodied the tone of society drama. He was more at ease with the society he depicted and on the whole less troubled by its codes of conduct. Pinero was frequently more searching and acknowledged those sordid and seedy aspects of what was for Jones a world of glitter. Pinero, for instance, examined the legal consequences of what in Jones's work are merely elopements with romantic overtones. In *The Benefit of the Doubt* (1895) and *Mid-Channel* (1909) the unpleasantness of divorce proceedings is made more powerful than the horror of ostracism from a round of polite social engagements. Jones's best work was done by the turn of the century; Pinero continued to experiment with established formulas throughout the first decade of the twentieth century. But by the end of that decade the dramatic work of Galsworthy, Granville Barker, and Shaw provided an indication that the drama, whilst still depending on many of the certainties of society drama, could go beyond them. Pinero's own *Mid-Channel* provided a swan-song for a style of drama he and Jones had created almost twenty years previously. The pronouncements of the *raisonneur*, Peter Mottram, are sententious, hollow, unconvincing; he has lost credibility as an authoritative commentator and is no longer an effective controller of human affairs. Catastrophe cannot be averted. As events in Europe after 1914 were to demonstrate, it would be difficult to believe in a universe which benignly directed the affairs of Edwardian England.

Galsworthy

John Galsworthy was born in 1867 at Kingston Hill, Surrey into a wealthy and very comfortable upper-middle-class family. His father was a practising solicitor who accumulated a six-figure fortune through directorships in various companies and land and property speculation. In accordance with his social and economic background Galsworthy was educated by private governesses until the age of nine, followed by preparatory school at Bournemouth, then Harrow, and New College, Oxford where, his father intending him for the Bar, he read law. For a man who was later to be seen as a satirical scourge of the upper middle classes, little in his educational career suggested anything but compliance with behavioural codes accepted of a man of his background. On leaving Oxford, Galsworthy was set for a career in fashionable legal and commercial spheres, and was called to the Bar in 1890. His involvement in these circles was leisurely and in many respects his life was not so different from the lives of the fashionable professional men inhabiting the society drama of Jones and Pinero.

His inclination to be a writer seems, initially at least, to have been similarly dilettantish. In a letter of 1894 he yearned, 'I do wish I had the gift of writing, I really think that is the nicest way of making money going' (Marrot, p. 97). Galsworthy set about the task of producing fiction and *From the Four Winds*, a collection of short stories published at his own expense, appeared in 1897. This was followed by two novels, *Jocelyn* in 1898 and *Villa Rubein* in 1900, and a collection of four long stories, *A Man of Devon*, published in 1901. At this time Galsworthy resigned from the Bar in order to devote his time to becoming a professional writer. Between 1901 and 1904 he published nothing, but he laboured assiduously to acquire the skills of a novelist. The results were *The Island Pharisees* in 1904 and *The Man of Property* in 1906.

Galsworthy's early writing career indicates a crucial difference from that of Jones and Pinero. The scope and style of their early work were dictated by the rigorous demands of the commercial theatre, and once they became professional dramatists what they wrote had to be continually acceptable to that theatre if they were to make a living. Galsworthy's private income buffered him from such necessity and allowed a three year period during which he published nothing whilst, drafting and redrafting, he learned his craft. Even more importantly, as his livelihood was not dependent upon his writing, royalties were not his primary consideration. When he tried his hand at writing plays he deliberately eschewed the sort of drama which brought such handsome rewards to dramatists like Jones and Pinero.

By 1906, the year in which Galsworthy completed his first play *The Silver Box*, much pioneering work had been done in the cause of the minority theatre, and the concept of such a theatre and the nature of its drama was well established. On the instigation of his literary mentor, Edward Garnett, Galsworthy's play was specifically written for performance at the Court where the Vedrenne–Barker seasons were in their third season. Galsworthy claimed in a letter of 1913, 'I think I may say (without exaggeration) that I came into theatre-land quite free from the influence of any dramatist or any kind of stage writing' (Marrot, p. 714). His claim, however, is something of an exaggeration. Galsworthy was consciously writing for a theatre conceived of as providing an alternative to the values of the commercial theatre not least in its expectations of the sort of realistic drama it presented. His letters before the staging of *The Silver Box* indicate that he was fully aware of the nature of both the actor managers' and the minority theatres, and had a knowledge of the work of specific playwrights, actors, and drama critics. Nor should his relationship with Garnett, whose extensive commentary and advice on early drafts of Galsworthy's work was often followed by the aspiring writer, be overlooked. Garnett was himself a dramatist working specifically in the minority theatre and the banning of his play *The*

Breaking Point (1907), because the plot concerned an unmarried woman's pregnancy and suicide, was to place him fully in a central concern of the minority theatre.

Galsworthy's intention was to produce a drama which would shun what he called 'the cursed convention' (Galsworthy, 1934, p. 130) of contemporary drama. Although his attack is specifically levied at Pinero's *His House in Order*, his comment indicates more generally his distaste for the conventions and strategies of society drama. In his own work this entailed a shift away from the dominant belief that the upper middle classes constituted the legitimate material for a serious drama of modern life; and those contrivances of plot and the workings of fortuitous coincidence, which bring about appropriate resolutions, were also to be avoided. Given Galsworthy's general predisposition as a writer, it is hardly surprising to discover that in his remarks on his drama he shows a commitment to the concepts of environmental naturalism. The conventions of naturalism would, he believed, create an authentic relationship between life and the stage which was lacking in the strategies of the society drama. This was a belief he held throughout his writing career, but, as we shall see, he rarely resolved the theoretical contradictions of the positions he adopted.

At his most extreme Galsworthy adhered without qualification to the concept of the 'fourth wall': 'With plays . . . it is only a question of the "fourth wall"; if you have a subject of sufficient dramatic interest, and visualize it powerfully enough, perfectly naturally, as if you were the fourth wall, you will be able to present it to others in the form of a good play' (Marrot, p. 565). As always, the 'fourth wall' metaphor is unsatisfactory as an explanation of the method of realist drama both in terms of the drama's formal structuring and the practicalities of its staging. Galsworthy himself elsewhere qualified this idea. The aim of the dramatist is 'to set before the public no cut-and-dried codes, but the phenomena of life and character, selected and combined, *but not distorted*, by the dramatist's outlook, set down without fear, favour, or prejudice, leaving the public to draw such poor moral as nature may afford' (Galsworthy, 1912, p. 190). He expresses an aversion to drama as having a palpable intent upon its audience and to the playwright as instrumental in supporting discernible social and moral codes. The dramatist, Galsworthy realized, must select and order his material, but the ultimate aim must be scientific impartiality and objectivity. Here he is in accordance with a central tenet of naturalist theory. 'In the whole range of the social fabric,' he added in the same essay, 'there are only two impartial persons, the scientist and the artist' (Galsworthy, 1912, p. 193). Galsworthy begs as many questions as does the 'fourth wall' analogy.

Galsworthy, in other qualifications of the notion of a documentary naturalism, comes closer to his actual practice:

> My own method was the outcome of the trained habit (which I was already employing in my novels) of naturalistic dialogue guided, informed, and selected by a controlling idea, together with an intense visualisation of types and scenes. I just wrote down the result of these two, having always in my mind's eye not the stage, but the room or space where in real life the action would pass. (Marrot, p. 714)

It is the 'idea', that is the cohesive ideology of the dramatist himself, which controls and informs the drama. The hierarchical importance of the 'idea' as the shaping principle of a drama is implicit in Galsworthy's phrase 'a spire of meaning': 'A drama must be shaped so as to have a spire of meaning. Every grouping of life and character has its inherent moral; and the business of the dramatist is so to pose the group as to bring that moral poignantly to the light of day' (Galsworthy, 1912, p. 189). The precise nature of the controlling idea is illuminated by his preface to the collected plays:

> To deal austerely and naturalistically with the life of one's day is to find the human being so involved in environment that he cannot be disassociated . . . [My characters] are part of the warp and woof of a complicated society, in which the individual is as much netted-in by encircling fates as ever were the creations of Greek dramatists. (Galsworthy, 1923–9, XVIII, pp. xii–xiii)

This adaptation of the concept of an environmental naturalism dependent on the immediate setting (suggested by the 'fourth wall' analogy or 'the room or space where in real life the action would pass') is crucial, for it becomes clear that it is the workings of society in a more generalized and abstract sense which orders the action of the plays and determines their plotting strategies. The 'idea' which becomes the dominant ordering principle in Galsworthy's drama is in fact his preconceived understanding of how society works, an understanding determined by his own ideological position – that of a reforming liberal.

Yet several of Galsworthy's Edwardian plays are superficially reminiscent of the society drama. *Joy* (1907), with its country house setting, its depiction of a way of life dependent on the dividends of conservative investment, and its presentation of a morally irregular liaison between Mrs Gwynn, estranged from her husband, and Maurice Lever, an interloper figure, deals with material which would have been thoroughly familiar to audiences who knew their Jones and Pinero. There is, however, a difference, and it lies in Galsworthy's treatment. The experience mediated is radically different from that of society drama. Unlike the world of Jones's society comedies, where the characters are given incomes which render any concern about money irrelevant, the dividends upon which Colonel and Mrs Hope exist in impoverished gentility are pitifully small and a cause of constant irritation and perplexity. Strong and complex plotting, arranged to arrive at a conventionally moral resolution, does not figure. There is public exposure neither of the relationship between Lever and Mrs Gwynn nor of the side issue of Lever's involvement in a dubious share flotation. Lever and Mrs Gwynn remain together at the end of the play, and what is asserted is her right to self-determination and self-fulfilment over and above orthodox social, marital, and maternal obligations. No *raisonneur* figure presides over the play. Colonel Hope, whose social position would make him a suitable candidate, is tentative, timid, and ineffectual. The play mostly works through the creation of a pervasive twilight atmosphere of enervation and decrepitude. Country house society has been left behind by an economic order it can neither control nor understand and is confronted by a sexual morality of which it disapproves but can do nothing about.

Elements of *The Fugitive* (1913) – a wife's coldness towards a prosaic husband and the presence of an interloper who compromises her virtue and reputation – take up similar themes to Jones's *The Liars* and *The Case of Rebellious Susan*. But its plot structure represents a radical revision of society drama's practice. Unlike the resolutions of Jones's plays where the last acts show the return of errant wives to the safety of their husbands, Clare, the fugitive of the title, leaves her husband at the end of the first act and the remainder of the play charts her progress from marital respectability to shop girl, to kept mistress, to prostitution.

As with *Joy*, it is not so much the material which marks the play as belonging to the minority theatre but Galsworthy's plotting strategies and the emphasis of his treatment. The play does not provide a role in which the actor manager can project an acceptable image; the part of Malise, the interloper, was offered to Gerald du Maurier, but he considered the character to be 'unbearable, a carper, a sneerer, and a bore' (Marrot, p. 371). Moreover, there is an acerbity in Galsworthy's depiction of the institution of marriage. It is presented not as ultimately sacrosanct, though never-so fraught, as in the society drama, but as an economic arrangement where a woman's compliance with dominant gender obligations of duty and obedience, including the sexual relationship, are tokens of barter, value for goods received. Galsworthy repeats the same idea in the last act as Clare, about to embark on a life of prostitution, negotiates with a potential client. The equivalence established between the two areas of sexual relationships constitutes an analysis of marriage that the gentlemanly tone of the society drama dared not countenance. Similarly, Jones may have paid lip service to the notion that the failure of Lady Susan's rebellion was a tragedy, but his play, like other society dramas, is implicitly instrumental in endorsing an economic and social order which makes women such as Clare and Lady Susan fit for nothing but to be the wives of wealthy men. *The Fugitive*, on the contrary, is in many ways a striking and unrelenting condemnation of those systems of oppression and their ratification by the power given to husbands by the divorce courts.

This is, of course, all to Galsworthy's credit. Yet the play remains in many of its implications reactionary. *The Fugitive* was seen as a sequel to *A Doll's House* in showing what happens to a Nora after she slams the door and walks out, and was considered by some to be a 'version more credible and realistic than the original' (Williams, p. 257). That sort of approval, in certain quarters, arose from the exemplary nature of Galsworthy's depiction of the stages in Clare's moral and social descent of which the last, prostitution, could be seen as especially fitting; 'the natural end of idleness and selfishness' (Marrot, p. 371), was du Maurier's opinion. Indeed, the inevitability of her career and the final gesture of suicide by which she escapes the ignominy of prostitution can be read as cautionary rather than exemplary. By showing the catastrophic results of her behaviour, *The Fugitive* at one level embodies the advice not to rebel which is explicit in the society drama. For despite the criticism and the play's pervasive sour tone, Galsworthy accepts as given the society drama's own formulations of woman's position and role. Unlike other Edwardian plays, Barrie's *The Twelve-Pound Look* (1910) and Houghton's *Hindle Wakes* (1912) for instance, Galsworthy's analysis of society's oppression of women cannot accommodate the existence of social, economic, or employment structures through which women can achieve a measure of economic independence or independence from male authority and protection.

Although economic referents and determinants are carefully worked into the play, the system which defines Clare is primarily moral. Like the women of society drama she is defined in terms of her roles as wife, mistress, and prostitute. Of the stages in Clare's path, these are the only roles in which she is presented on stage; she merely reports her experience as shop worker, which, of her various roles, represents economic independence and moral neutrality:

> Lots of the girls are really nice. But somehow they don't want me, can't help thinking I've got airs or something; and in here

(She touches her breast) I don't want them! . . . It's working *under* people; it's *having* to do it, being driven. I *have* tried, I've not been altogether a coward, really! But every morning getting there the same time; every day the same stale 'dinner', as they call it; every evening the same 'Good evening, Miss Clare,' 'Good evening, Miss Simpson,' 'Good evening, Miss Hart.' 'Good evening, Miss Clare.' And the same walk home, or the same bus; and the same men that you mustn't look at, for fear they'll follow you. (Act 3 Scene 1)

An opportunity is here provided for Galsworthy to indulge his predilection for drawing attention to matters of current social concern, in this instance manifested in late Victorian and Edwardian attempts to introduce legislative reform of the working conditions of shop assistants. But he is less exercised over the experience and effects of work than, as the close of the speech indicates, notions of male protection. *The Fugitive* modulates a set of familiar theatrical conventions which could mediate the consequences of moral impropriety more effectively than the experience of economic independence. Galsworthy, like Jones and Pinero, was indebted to the ethical intonations and attendant emotional structure of earlier melodrama.

The Eldest Son (1912), despite its upper-middle-class country house setting, in part announces its commitment to a minority drama by presenting working-class characters who are central to the action of the drama in a way which is not the case with *Joy*, *The Fugitive*, or the dominant mode of society drama. The play's central issue is that Freda Studdenham, maid to Lady Cheshire, is pregnant after an entanglement with Bill, the eldest son of the Cheshire family. A parallel case is introduced. Dunning, an underkeeper to Sir William Cheshire, has placed a village girl, Rose, in the same predicament. This strategy provides a central interest for the play by allowing Galsworthy to demonstrate the social and moral implications of the discrepancy between Sir William's treatment of his son and heir and his treatment of his employee, Dunning. Bill is forbidden from marrying Freda on pain of losing his inheritance; Dunning must marry Rose on pain of losing his job. Galsworthy uses the structural parallelism in order to expose the hypocrisy and hollow posturing of the upper middle classes. Through the relativism of Sir William's moral stances Galsworthy propounds his concept of the tactics by which 'society' (that is to say one very small section of society) enforces control and maintains its own power.

To this end the presence of the working-class characters – Dunning, Rose, Freda and Studdenham, her father – is essentially functional. The dramatic centre of the play lies in an examination of the attitudes and ways of living of the dominant class. The possibility of a marriage between Bill and Freda is of consequence only in so far as it will affect him and his family; similarly, when the conclusion of the play releases him from his proposal, the emphasis allows for no real consideration of what Freda's position will be as an unmarried mother. Galsworthy's treatment may differ from that of the society drama, but it embodies the same proposal that material interesting and significant enough for a serious drama of modern life is only to be found in the upper classes. Galsworthy is able to find a mode of dramatic writing which allows a detailed mediation of the foundations of the assumptions and habits of thinking of the Cheshire family and the class they represent, but the function of working-class characters as devices to that end means that little attempt is made to examine the basis of working-class behaviour or thinking. Studdenham, Freda's father, for instance, is forthright in his refusal of a loveless charity marriage for his daughter:

> We want none of you! She'll not force herself where she's not welcome. She may ha' slipped her good name, but she'll keep her proper pride. I'll have no *charity marriage* in my family . . . (*He takes hold of Freda, and looks around him.*) Well! She's not the first this has happened to since the world began, an' she won't be the last. Come away, now, come away! (Act 3)

This owes little to any mediation within the play of the formations of working-class culture and moral attitudes, but a great deal to a conventional image of integrity, honesty, steadfastness, and communal solidarity frequently attributed to the common people in nineteenth-century domestic melodrama. In relation to this system of class, gender, and moral definition, *The Eldest Son* achieves many of its effects. Ultimately, Studdenham's attitude provides a convenient structural conclusion to Galsworthy's primary purpose of highlighting upper-middle-class hypocrisy. But, more problematically, it resolves the issue raised by the relationship between Bill and Freda in a way which would not have been unpalatable to the society drama. Bill goes admonished but unpunished, Freda, like many of the morally lapsed before her, simply disappears. The Cheshire blood, and thus the established social order, survives unthreatened by possible miscegenation with the lower orders.

If *Joy*, *The Fugitive*, and *The Eldest Son*, despite the treatment of the material, show some affinity with the society drama, it is Galsworthy's use in *The Silver Box*, *Justice* (1910), and *Strife* (1909), of different areas of subject matter and the more central placing of working-class characters, which significantly marks the latter plays as claiming an affinity with the minority drama.

In *The Silver Box*, Galsworthy explores similar themes and exploits a similar technique to those of *The Eldest Son*. At the opening of the play, Jones, an unemployed groom, and young Barthwick, son of a wealthy Liberal MP, commit parallel petty thefts. Both are drunk when the offences are committed. Barthwick has stolen the purse of a young woman with whom he has been spending the evening. Jones, having helped Barthwick home, steals a silver cigarette box and the young woman's purse. The motivation for the thefts is identical — a spiteful desire to score off the victim. Once this parallelism is established, the course of the play demonstrates a world of difference in the way the two are dealt with by the legal process and courts of law. At the end of the play Barthwick's crime goes undetected, Jones ends up with a month's hard labour. That there is one law for the rich and another for the poor is unequivocally asserted.

As in *The Eldest Son*, Galsworthy exposes the working of a double standard. However, unlike the double standard of society drama, sexual morality is not necessarily Galsworthy's concern. The double standard of his play is defined not by gender but by class and wealth. Barthwick's money can prevent the exposure of his son's crime by buying off his lady friend and thereby avoiding prosecution. The Barthwicks immediately call in the police over the business of the silver box and put in motion the process of law. Suspicion falls on Jones's wife who chars for the Barthwicks, and when the police visit her home they discover the stolen property brought home not by her but her husband. Both are arrested for the theft. The problem for the Barthwicks now is that the discovery of the stolen purse could implicate their son and his own crime when Jones is examined before the magistrate. The last act, set in the magistrate's court, is a remarkable achievement for a first play, and in it Galsworthy draws together his themes and exposes the administration of the double standard. The Barthwicks' appearance of respectability, a correlative of their social and economic standing, automatically predisposes the magistrate in their favour; the opposite is, of course, the case with Jones. Additionally, Barthwick's money enables him to engage a clever solicitor who effectively manipulates the proceedings so that the connection between young Barthwick's crime and Jones's does not come to light. Jones, legally unrepresented, hardly gets a fair hearing.

The parallelism of the plot structure, as with that of *The Eldest Son*, throws the central dramatic emphasis onto the attitudes and implicit hypocrisies of the upper middle class who countenance and perpetuate the double standard. Galsworthy, however, is careful not to create villains out of Barthwick, the magistrate, or Roper, Barthwick's solicitor. Barthwick is more weak than wicked; it is simply that his sympathies for the plight of the poor and his professions of principle crumble when they come into conflict with self-interest. Roper is the truly culpable man. Fully apprised by the facts in both cases, he conceals the truth in one of them and exploits the unthinking class-conscious prejudices of the magistrate. Yet his culpability is meant to be offset by his own ironic perception of the advantages of wealth and class, and his position as the family solicitor is presented as entailing certain obligations to his client. Unwittingly rather than deliberately the magistrate allows a verdict which endorses his prejudices.

The relationships of power and class are not dissimilar from those of a long tradition of Victorian melodrama. But Galsworthy's strategy, in the depiction of figures from the dominant class, eschews the intonation of melodrama by indicting a system of prejudice rather than a set of villainous individuals. Jones, however, is defined more specifically by the moral and emotional structures of melodrama, especially those of temperance melodrama. His poverty and his experience of unemployment, though spelt out by Galsworthy as contributory factors in his crime, become subordinated to an ethical definition arising from his drunkenness. Like the protagonists of temperance melodrama, Jones's lamentable economic state is more the result of than the cause of his drinking. And, like those protagonists, he is judged by the extent to which his drinking results in the desecration of the domestic ideal. Familiar images of violence in the home, weeping children, and the literal sundering of the family unit result in an emotional intonation dependent on this central defining system of domestic melodrama. In *The Silver Box*, Galsworthy seems incapable of going beyond this method of defining his working-class characters. At the beginning of the court scene, a case of another unemployed man, Livens, comes before the magistrate. He represents a point of comparison to Jones:

LIVENS: (*Ashamedly*) My wife, she broke my 'ome up, and pawned the things.
MAGISTRATE: But what made you let her?
LIVENS: Your Worship, I'd no chance to stop 'er; she did it when I was out lookin' for work.
MAGISTRATE: Did you ill-treat her?
LIVENS: (*Emphatically*) I never raised my 'and to her in my life, your Worship.
MAGISTRATE: Then what was it – did she drink?
LIVENS: Yes, your Worship. (Act 3)

Galsworthy seems eager to emphasize that unemployment and depravity, as evidenced in the case of Jones, are not necessarily correlatives. But Mrs Livens takes on the role of protagonist in the temperance melodrama and the cause of the Livens's destitution is drink rather than unemployment. This is in many ways unfortunate for it reinforces the discriminatory class-determined systems of definition Galsworthy employs in the play. By establishing the parallel between Jones and young Barthwick, Galsworthy may expose the class-consciousness of the magistrate; the latter smiles at the fact of Barthwick's drinking too much champagne but takes a much sterner view of Jones's drunkenness. But it is a system of prejudice to which Galsworthy himself implicitly subscribes. Young Barthwick may be presented as a wastrel and a cad yet he never, even when drunk, descends to the viciousness and violence central to Galsworthy's concept of Jones.

Galsworthy does, however, utilize some types of ethical definition in ideologically more interesting ways. The fact that Mrs Jones gave birth to their first child before marriage does not give rise to the irrevocable condemnation in melodrama and society drama. Galsworthy uses the opportunity, primarily through the attitudes of Mrs Barthwick, to expose that prejudicial, and ultimately hypocritical, system of moral judgement. Moreover, Mrs Jones's history and present condition, like those of Ruth Honeywill in *Justice*, present her as a victim not just of the demon drink but specifically of marital oppression and male brutality.

The traditions of domestic and temperance melodrama which Galsworthy utilizes in the definition of Jones and Mrs Livens are extended and their capacity for powerful emotional response harnessed in a deft move consonant with Galsworthy's desire to examine the operation of institutional formations. The disapprobation which adheres to those who desecrate domestic ideals goes beyond specific individuals, for the destruction of the family unit is in both cases compounded by the impersonal agencies of legal and judicial processes. The magistrate, with some reluctance, makes a court order for Livens's children to be taken from their father and placed in care. The fate of the family is determined by what is presented as the constraints of the magistrate's and Relieving Officer's remit and duty, but the effect is to complete the disintegration of the Livens family initiated by Mrs Livens. The emotional intensity of the incident is enhanced by the stage image of two small, ragged children in the large and imposing courtroom eventually being physically escorted away by a uniformed policeman. The lachrymatory potential of small children in melodrama is elsewhere fully exploited by Galsworthy, but again is located within his social concerns. Mrs Jones's son, unable to find her after her arrest, comes in search of her to the Barthwick home and, unseen, sobs piteously outside the window. The child's plight is occasioned specifically because Barthwick has put the machinery of the law into operation by calling in the police, and the play makes clear that, no matter what the personal feelings of the Barthwicks now are, the matter is consequently beyond their control. Galsworthy's emotionalism borders on sentimentality, yet he defended the incident in a letter to Edward Garnett. 'I keep the child's crying, because a physical thrill to the audience at this point is worth any added Barthwick psychology. You know my theory (founded on personal experience) that the physical emotional thrill is all that really counts in a play' (Galsworthy, 1934, p. 17). The relationship between the emotional and intellectual structures of Galsworthy's plays is far closer to that of the society drama than either the elliptical cerebrality of Granville-Barker or the ideational barnstorming of Shaw.

Galsworthy returned to the theme of the legal process in *Justice*. The episodic structure of this play provides a series of settings which enable an examination of various aspects of the judicial system. It opens in James Howe's solicitors' office, moves to a law court, presents a montage of scenes in a prison, and for its close returns to the solicitors' office. The central figure, Falder, is a junior clerk in the law firm. He forges a cheque so that he can emigrate with Ruth Honeywill whom he loves but who is married to a drunken husband who illtreats her. The forgery is discovered and the next two acts are concerned with his treatment by the law courts and the effect upon him of imprisonment, particularly solitary confinement. The last act takes place two years later and is concerned with his plight as an ex-convict. Falder has been released on parole and returns to the office to ask to be re-engaged. He has, however, broken the terms of his parole by failing to report regularly to the police and, to circumvent prejudices against ex-convicts, has previously gained employment by using forged references. When a policeman arrives inquiring after him he commits suicide to avoid re-arrest and re-imprisonment.

As in *The Silver Box*, it is not individuals who are indicted but a system of judgement and punishment which is relentless and inexorable. James Howe, the solicitor, the judge, and learned counsels, are merely servants of the law. The law is a force in itself, inviolable and self-validating, comprising a set of principles over and above individual feeling or sympathy. Similarly, the administrators of the prison system are well meaning. But they can only operate within the limitations of their official brief. The standards of that brief are arbitrary and cannot accommodate or take heed of the specific case that Falder represents without disrupting the system as a whole.

Counsel for the defence not only predicts the outcome of the play but spells out its 'spire of meaning':

> Gentlemen, men like the prisoner are destroyed daily under our law for want of that human insight which sees them as they are, patients, and not criminals. If the prisoner be found guilty, and treated as though he were a criminal type, he will, as all experience shows, in all probability become one. I beg you not to return a verdict that may thrust him back into prison and brand him for ever. Gentlemen, Justice is a machine that, when someone has once given it the starting push, rolls on of itself. Is this young man to be ground to pieces under this machine for an act which at the worst was one of weakness? Is he to become a member of the luckless crews that man those dark, ill-starred ships called prisons? Is that to be his voyage – from which so few return? Or is he to have another chance, to be still looked on as one who has gone a little astray, but who will come back? I urge you, gentlemen, do not ruin this young man! (Act 2)

Counsel's urging is not heeded.

Comparison is often made between *Justice* and Tom Taylor's melodrama *The Ticket-of-Leave Man* (1863) which also engages with the problems facing ex-convicts. The differences are instructive. Bob Brierly, the hero of Taylor's play, is subjectively innocent of the crime for which he is imprisoned and is more the victim of the villains of the piece than of either society or institutional forces. The relationship between the plot and ethical structures of melodrama is such that prison is the making of him. It cures him of his incipient dipsomania and provides him with skills for future life and employment. He is a model prisoner and, once he has effected the capture of the villains, it is taken for granted that he will be a model citizen. May Edwards, who patiently waits for him, is able by the exercise of the principles of self-help to establish herself in lower-middle-class comfort so as to provide a home for him on his release. The social and economic formations of Galsworthy's world are fundamentally more hostile. Ruth Honeywill is forced into becoming another man's kept mistress in order to survive whilst Falder is in prison. And the effect of prison on Falder is to break him as a man. It merely compounds the inherent weakness of his character and renders him useless as a future member of society. Prison is not reformist but recidivistic.

The case for recidivism is stressed by interviews with other prisoners in the third act of the play as well as by counsel for the defence, yet its principal proof resides in Falder's career and eventual fate. There is, however, a danger that Galsworthy is arguing too much from the specific to the general. As with Clare's similar entrapment by social forces in *The Fugitive* or the thesis of one law for the rich another for the poor of *The Eldest Son* and *The Silver Box*, it is not the case that Galsworthy's perceptions are necessarily wrong. Rather the plays tend to be too bludgeoning in their tendentiousness, take too little account of the complexities and contradictions within the very social, economic, and political formations they set out to explore. Falder is as much a pawn of Galsworthy's didacticism as he is victim of the legal system.

The plotting, especially the close parallels in *The Eldest Son* and *The Silver Box*, constitutes a strategy as neat and totalizing as the techniques of the conventional well-made play utilized by the society drama. Despite Galsworthy's adherence to notions of fourth-wall naturalism and impartiality, his hand is clearly at work in the organization of the plays. The construction and the ideology, which create the mediated experience, impose an externally created sense of form, a coercive intellectual order, on the action and characters. The plays demonstrate the working out of certain *a priori* assumptions about the nature of Edwardian society and present a proof of the truths of those assumptions just as Jones and Pinero devised strategies to prove the truth of their *a priori* assumptions. All three dramatists contrive situations that, granted the assumptions of their ideological biases, must end in a certain way. Unlike the indeterminate endings of Granville Barker's *The Voysey Inheritance* and *The Madras House* (to be discussed in the next chapter), which are so organized to create the impression of a lack of imposed constructional form, the endings of Galsworthy's plays mediate a finality which is the QED of the initial assumptions which have ordered the action.

In order to demonstrate the nature of Falder's complete entrapment and prove points about the penal system, Galsworthy has to create a character who is acted upon, a character whose central traits are passivity and weakness. Such features are not necessarily approved of in the way that the stoic endurance of the heroes and heroines of domestic melodrama often is. But they are a necessary function both of Galsworthy's ideological position and the promotion of a set of emotional responses which supports that position. With the exception of Studdenham in *The Eldest Son* and Roberts in *Strife*, such features can be found in virtually all of the working-class characters in Galsworthy's pre-war plays. In order to illuminate his view of the unfairness and injustice of vertical hierarchies of power and class in Edwardian Britain, not only are individual working-class characters presented as passive and weak; working-class life, consonant with the determinism of literary naturalism, has to be wretched, oppressed, and at heart joyless. Even though Galsworthy introduces working people into central positions in the drama and, according to his lights, treats them seriously and compassionately, the tendentious nature of the plays can provide only a partial view of their lives.

There is a certain irony, given Galsworthy's liberal reforming instincts, that the structuring of his plays admits less possibility of change than the conservatism of the society drama of Jones and

Pinero. The inbuilt ideological assumptions of society drama and the dominance of the *raisonneur* result in denouements which maintain established social and moral forms; but a fundamental initial premise upon which society drama is built is that people are capable of making individual choices about their lives. Many of the underlying tensions in the drama arise from the acknowledgement that those choices can challenge and indeed change the order of society. Galsworthy's drama proposes that people, even those who administer the system, are in the last resort unable to make any effective intervention in the workings of institutional and social forces. There is a further irony, given the impotence of all the characters in *Justice*, that the play is one of the very few literary works which has provoked actual legislative change. Largely through the power of a scene in dumbshow, which shows Falder in solitary confinement pacing his cell like a caged animal until he finally flings himself against the door and desperately beats it with his fists, Winston Churchill, then recently appointed as Home Secretary, undertook a series of prison reforms which included a reduction of the period of mandatory solitary confinement. The effect of *Justice* is a telling indicator of the construction of social formations in Galsworthy's drama. They have an autonomous power which makes them unassailable within the plays themselves. The implicit message of the plays is that an amelioration of injustices in society can only be effected by those, external to the plays, whom society itself has endowed with the power to bring about official or legislative reform.

Strife, a drama of an industrial dispute, represents both a confirmation and a variation on the methods of Galsworthy's other plays. The action takes place on the last day of a long running strike in a tin-plate works on the Welsh border. The men and their families, literally being starved out, are in a pitiable condition, and the members of the board are concerned for their dividends. There is a feeling on both sides that a compromise should be arrived at so as to end the strike. This, however, is blocked by the intransigence of the two leaders – Roberts for the men and Anthony for the masters. Their obduracy has kept their wavering supporters together and prolonged the strike, but during the course of the play they gradually lose their authority. The death of Mrs Roberts, brought on by malnutrition, is a decisive catalyst for both sides. The two leaders, still willing to fight it out, are outvoted by their followers and an agreement is reached. The whole business turns out to have been ironically futile; at the close of the play the company secretary points out, 'These terms, they're the *very same* we drew up together, you and I, and put to both sides before the fight began' (Act 3).

The oppositional nature of the industrial dispute allows Galsworthy to exploit a series of parallels in much the same way as in *The Eldest Son* and *The Silver Box*. By an almost cinematic intercutting between analogous scenes showing the two sides of the dispute he establishes parallel developments in plot. Most importantly, the technique proves the stances of the two leaders to be in essence identical. The same is true of their eventual downfall. This strategy is central to Galsworthy's belief in the value of impartiality. By utilizing a series of juxtaposed parallels he purports to be setting down 'without fear, favour, or prejudice' both sides of the case. Whether the play manages to maintain this level of intellectual impartiality is questionable. What is undeniable is that any pretension to an overall impartiality is nullified by Galsworthy's manipulation of the emotional structure of the play. Parallelism requires that there should be scenes in both the manager's and Roberts' homes. But the juxtaposition of luxury in the manager's house (well-provisioned with food, drink and fuel) and the Roberts', where Mrs Roberts is dying of starvation and down to her last coals, is not neutral. Galsworthy's strategy is deliberately designed to create an emotional pattern of sympathy and pity for the workers. Conversely, the subjects of conversation amongst the board members – the quality of the food at the local hotel, a desire to resolve things quickly so a certain train can be caught – make them seem petty and mean-spirited in contrast to the real hardships the workers are suffering. The emotional structure, as in his other plays, is a function of Galsworthy's overview of the position of the working class in Edwardian society. Above all, what the dispute offends is Galsworthy's sense of fair play. The material advantages of the board mean that the fight is not a fair one, and Galsworthy organizes the play so that the audience will share his sense of inequity.

Strife differs from plays like *Justice* and *The Silver Box* in that the inevitability of its outcome does not arise from the ineluctability of social, economic, or institutional formations. The drama crystallizes into a clash between the two leaders as individuals. Their psychological dispositions, when brought into conflict, result in what Galsworthy saw as the tragedy of the play. This emphasis in the treatment subordinates the strategies of naturalistic convention which he elsewhere employs. Of all his pre-war plays, *Strife* is Galsworthy's most direct examination of class and political conflict. But details central to the depiction of the conflict, such as social and economic referents and the mediation of class-determined political positions and cultural attitudes, operate less as devices which actively define the drama than as framework for the action. Such details represent a technique of a mode of dramatic writing which superficially rather than functionally authenticates the action in an equivalent way to the representational sets of realistic staging.

The central impetus in determining the outcome of the play is founded upon the fluctuating levels of *personal* support for the two leaders; and the eventual outcome is essentially an issue of *personal* betrayal. Consequently, even though several scenes in the play are taken up with formal meetings, actual details of the strike, for instance its cause, remain indistinct. In keeping with the emotional structure of the play, the material plight of the men and their families is the paramount issue in all the discussions. This may make better sentimental drama, but it is dangerously close to violating the principles of close observation and factuality upon which the realism of Galsworthy's drama is predicated. The structuring and emphasis of the play render the precise details of the strike immaterial as is the validity of the case of either side.

The oppositional nature of the conflict central to *Strife* results in the airing of arguments central to the organization of capitalist society. Here is Anthony on his fight against labour:

It has been said that masters and men are equal! Cant! There can only be one master in a house! Where two men meet the better will rule. It has been said that Capital and Labour have the same interests. Cant! Their interests are as wide asunder as the poles. It has been said that the Board is only part of a machine. Cant! We *are* the machine; its brains and sinews; it is for us to lead and to determine what is to be done, and to do it without fear or favour . . . There is only one way of treating 'men' – with *the iron hand* . . . Masters are masters, men are men! . . . I am thinking of the future of this country, threatened with the black waters of confusion, threatened with mob government, threatened with what I cannot see. If by any conduct of mine I help to bring this on us, I shall be ashamed to look my fellows in the face. (Act 3)

And here is Roberts on his fight against capital:

The fight o' the country's body and blood against a bloodsucker. The fight of those that spend theirselves with every blow they strike and every breath they draw, against a thing that fattens on them, and grows and grows by the law of *merciful* Nature. That thing is Capital! A thing that buys the sweat o' men's brows, and the tortures o' their brains, at its own price . . . It is a thing that will take as much and give you as little as it can. That's *Capital*! . . . Tell me, for all their talk is there one of them that will consent to another penny on the Income Tax to help the poor? That's Capital! A white-faced, stony-hearted monster! (Act 2 Scene 2)

Yet the intrinsic validity of the political content of the statements is again largely immaterial. In addition to their contribution to the emotional temper of the play, their primary function is as tokens in its structural parallelism.

What I see as the really problematic result of Galsworthy's strategy is its denial of the validity, or even the possibility, of working-class political activism. The driving force behind the strike derives not from class solidarity, ideological commitment, or a sense of communal injustice but from Roberts' personal zeal.

In keeping with Galsworthy's general view of the passivity of working-class characters, Roberts' forcefulness necessitates his detachment from his class and fellow workers. The disclaimer of Enid Underwood, Anthony's daughter, that Roberts is not a common man like the other workers, 'I mean he's an engineer – a superior man' (Act 2 Scene 1), is typical of the thinking of a woman of her class and position. It is also very much Galsworthy's own view of Roberts. Roberts is quite deliberately disassociated from the other workers and made unrepresentative of those he leads.

With the exception of Roberts, the workers as a group are shown to be almost totally incapable of concerted political activity. The extent of Galsworthy's conviction of the impotence of the working class as a political force is indicated in a letter to Garnett. His conception for the play was that it is only Roberts' leadership which has led the workers' 'naturally sluggish and mediocre tempers to fight too long' (Galsworthy, 1934, p. 157). Galsworthy's overview of the working class may condition his treatment of the workers as a group even more than it does Roberts. But Roberts himself is not immune from the concept. The play gives credence to the notion that Roberts is motivated not solely by political principle and ideological commitment but by a sense of personal grievance and thus a desire for personal revenge. In this, Galsworthy presents Roberts' motivation in much the same way as that of Rushton, the Luddite agitator of John Walker's melodrama of industrial unrest *The Factory Lad* of 1832. And in both plays there is consequently that common and conventional tactic by which the political foundations of direct action can be deflected.

The defeats of both Roberts and Anthony at the end of *Strife* mark the final stage in the play's parallel structuring and mark also their complete isolation from those they previously led. In this isolation the two men are united in defeat. 'ANTHONY *rises with an effort. He turns to* ROBERTS, *who looks at him. They stand several seconds, gazing at each other fixedly;* ANTHONY *lifts his hand, as though to salute, but lets it fall. The expression of* ROBERTS' *face changes from hostility to wonder. They bend their heads in token of respect*' (Act 3). In their mutual recognition there is what Galsworthy intends to be a sense of shared common humanity. The two men are thus effectively detached from the social context which had earlier separated them. Differences of class, culture, and politics disappear as a means of defining their their identity or their relationship. The evidence of the play and Galsworthy's own conception of it concur:

> It has always been the fashion to suppose that it is a play on the subject of capital and labour. But the strike, which forms the staple material of the play, was only chosen by me as a convenient vehicle to carry the play's real theme which is that of the Greek υβρις, or violence; *Strife* is, indeed, a play on extremism or fanaticism . . . People who go to *Strife* expecting Capital or Labour to get a hoist are in for a disappointment. And people who go to *Strife* to see a photographic reproduction of an industrial struggle of to-day will come away saying that this, that, or the other is not true to life. But I suggest that people shouldn't go to *Strife* to see any such things. They should go to *Strife* to see human nature in the thick of a fight, the 'heroism' of diehardism, and the nemesis that dogs it. (Marrot, pp. 637–8)

In its range of subject matter and its central contentions, Galsworthy's Edwardian drama is clearly committed to the minority theatre. But as a whole it is ordered as clearly as the society drama by the author's ideological position and by the limitations of his understanding of the social and political forma-tions of Edwardian England.

IV
Granville Barker

Harley Granville Barker was born in 1877 in Kensington Town. Very little is known of his early life. Apart from the fact that in 1891 he spent some six months at Sarah Thorne's theatre school in Margate there is no other evidence of Barker's education, formal or otherwise. On his birth certificate his father's occupation is entered as 'Gentleman'. His mother was a professional performer – a reciter of popular poems and imitator of birdsong. As a child Barker was often included in the act. By 1895 he was a member of Ben Greet's touring company, playing in the kinds of sentimental and comic pieces which were the stock in trade of the mid and late Victorian stage: for example, James Albery's *Two Roses* (1870), Bulwer Lytton's *Money* (1840), and *Masks and Faces* (1852) by Tom Taylor and Charles Reade. He also played Romeo for Greet.

Unlike the other dramatists under discussion, Barker came from a family connected with the stage, albeit in a small way, and his initial career was in professional theatre. His first attempts at playwriting were in collaboration with Berte Thomas, whom Barker had met as a fellow student in Margate. Their extant *oeuvre* comprises three plays, *The Family of the Olroyds* (1895–6), *The Weather-Hen* (1897), and *Our Visitor to 'Work-a-day'* (1898–9). Only the second was to reach the stage. Unlike Jones, Pinero, and Galsworthy, Barker did not give up another occupation to become a full-time writer. Throughout the period before the First World War he continued to work as a professional actor and director. Like many performers committed in principle to the advanced drama he was compelled to act in the commercial theatre in order to make a living (he appeared in several revivals of Pinero's work), but his major achievement on stage was the creation of several of the major Shavian roles. Indeed Barker's most outstanding contribution to the Edwardian theatre was arguably as director and campaigner for the repertory movement, rather than as playwright. It is only following the seminal work by Margery Morgan and Gerald Weal that his drama has acquired the reputation it so thoroughly deserves.

The first play written by Granville Barker without the aid of Berte Thomas was *The Marrying of Ann Leete*. Completed in 1899, it was produced by the Stage Society in 1902. It is set in the late eighteenth century and for the most part takes place in the garden of the country home of Carnaby Leete, a failing politician. Thematically the play is dominated by images of sterility and degeneration whilst the plot hinges upon Leete's devious and cynical political machinations. The public world of political duplicity and the emotional sterility of the Leetes and their circle are concomitant. Leete has, before the play begins, condemned his eldest daughter, Sarah, to a hollow marriage to further his own political ends by enabling his move from the Whigs to the Tories. During the course of the play, he contrives to marry Ann to Lord John Carp in new scheming to expedite his return to the Whigs. The play presents Leete's engineering of political marriages as a distortion of natural affection and impulse. Ann rejects her father's political manoeuvring and defies social convention by proposing marriage to the gardener, John Abud. Their match asserts a symbolic return of vitality to a sterility which dominates social and political life.

The resolution of the play, the marriage of Abud and Ann Leete, is didactic, but not in any sense that it offers a practical solution to the sterility of the Leete world. Archibald Henderson, in 1927, criticized the ending of the play as a 'eugenic, but unnatural, solution of mating the overcivilized and devitalized woman with the coarse but pure-blooded man', and saw in it a 'strictly sociologic motive which might have occurred to Westermarck, but never to Anne Leete' (p. 389). (Alexander Westermarck, Professor of Sociology, University of London 1907–30; author of *The History of Marriage*, 1891.) *The Marrying of Ann Leete* can be seen in the context of larger contemporary fears of degeneration and ideas that the decline of the stock could be arrested by the injection of new blood. But, whilst Henderson's criticism is misguided in its assumption that the action of the play should be assessed by the standards of plausible realism, he does point to a very real tension in the play. The drama is largely mediated via the conventions of realist staging, but the play is not ultimately defined by the literal structure of society which the inter-class marriage of Abud and Ann Leete challenges. The marriage gains its real meaning from its function in the symbolic and metaphorical structure of the play. The collapse of social distinctions does not so much argue for a real reorganization of society as promote a certain construct of male vitality and sexuality. Masculinity is thus mythologized and presented as a sort of force beyond the limits of conventional society rather than, as it is in this particular manifestation, an expression of male domination inscribed in conventional society. In this respect, Barker renders Abud's class less significant than his profession. The gardener, concerned with germination and growth as his name somewhat heavy-handedly intimates, is a force for regeneration placed by Barker in symbolic opposition to the distortions of political and social inbreeding.

In terms of the play's symbolic system the presentation of Ann Leete herself becomes highly ambiguous. She is metaphorically as much a New Woman of the 1890s as she is a woman of the 1790s. Her proposal and marriage to Abud overturns social convention and gender expectations. She also exposes and confounds patriarchal oppression by rejecting Leete's plan to impose on her a socially acceptable and politically expedient marriage. Her independence and self-determination reside in that she, not her father, chooses whom she will marry. But more problematically, Barker does not allow her act to challenge the dominant marital construct of male dominance, proprietorship, and the husband's sexual rights, all of which are manifest in the final scene which is set in Abud's cottage on the wedding night. From the moment the couple enter the cottage and Abud locks the door behind them and hangs the key on its hook she has exchanged one form of oppression for another. Nevertheless, in terms of the symbolic system of the play Ann is validated and her decision vindicated by her potential for procreation.

Whilst *The Marrying of Ann Leete* may be defined by a body of ideas and a symbolic structure extrinsic to its social and historical setting, the play is neither dogmatic nor doctrinaire. The tone of the ending is fragile and uncertain, the marriage is represented by Barker as a hope for the future rather than as a conclusion. The plotting, with its rejection of a sense of a final ending is an affirmation of Barker's view of the couple's need to submit to a force which is beyond them. His technique is further characterized by the play's wandering and elliptical dialogue. The characters are thus prevented from being mouthpieces for the play's thematic concerns, nor are they pushed forward to act as sounding boards for its symbolism. The play avoids the overt tendentiousness imposed by the verbal explicitness, and the plotting and ideological strategies of society and Galsworthian drama.

On account of their contemporary settings, class structure, and subject matter, Barker's later plays, whilst prefigured in theme and method by *The Marrying of Ann Leete*, superficially seem adjacent to the work of Jones, Pinero, and Galsworthy. But it is through the very complexity of Barker's perception of Edwardian society and the subtlety of his technique that a very different experience is mediated.

The Voysey Inheritance (1905) presents a large late Victorian upper-middle-class family, seemingly typical in its solid respectability and financial security. Voysey, head of the household, is a fashionable and wealthy solicitor. His sons are not untypical in their professional roles: Trenchard, law; Booth, formerly army; Hugh, an artist; and Edward, the family firm. The surface of the play is firmly rooted in precise and concrete details of the ways of living mediated by the society drama. But the fact that the family firm is dishonest radically shifts the play's central dramatic focus and its system of definition. Voysey has used his clients' capital, entrusted to him for low-return but secure investment, to indulge for his own benefit in high-risk and more profitable stock. Barker is predominantly concerned with the ideological implications of that dishonesty.

At this point it may be worth noting that Pinero's play *Iris* also deals with the fraudulent use of investors' capital by an unscrupulous solicitor. But, characteristically, *Iris* does not suggest that the crime is anything other than an isolated case or that its cause lies anywhere else than in the dishonesty of one particular rogue. In *The Voysey Inheritance*, the dishonesty implicates not only the individual Voyseys but the institutions, ideology, and economic base of Edwardian England.

The play reverses the endorsement of conventional values which defined the society drama. Voysey's rejection of conventional codes of behaviour is presented as a sign of his vitality. His casting aside the trammels of the legal and financial systems becomes a form of heroism. The valedictory assessment of his peculiar talent made by Beatrice, Hugh's wife, is endorsed by the play: 'He was a great financier . . . a man of imagination. He had to find scope for his abilities or die. He despised these fat little clients living so snugly on their unearned incomes . . . and put them and their money to the best use he could' (Act 5). In putting money to its best use Voysey is the most effective capitalist in the play; his amorality implies an amorality fundamental to capitalism itself. Barker takes the logic of capitalist enterprise and uses it to invert the very ethical and legal codes which capitalist society invokes to protect and perpetuate its own structures.

The legal system is thus, according to Voysey, an artificial institution created to protect those who have grown weak and soft from living off inherited wealth and unearned income. Voysey's challenge to the mythologized economic basis of upper-middle-class life is summed up in the advice given to Alice Maitland by her guardian, a man of 'great character and no principles': 'He said once to me . . . You've no right to your money. You've not earned it or deserved it in any way. Therefore don't be surprised or annoyed if any enterprising person tries to get it from you. He has at least as much right to it as you have . . . if he can use it better, he has more right' (Act 3).

The polarities of Voysey's view are that 'You must either be the master of money or its servant' (Act 2). Voysey is validated within the play because he masterfully and actively manipulates money.

George Booth, a family friend and client, is money's servant and a stage direction stresses that he is merely passively dependent on his investments: '*Money has given him all he wants, therefore he loves and reverences money; while his imagination may be estimated by the fact that he has now reached the age of sixty-five, still possessing more of it than he knows what to do with*' (Act 2). George Booth is the substance on which the Voyseys batten. Unlike Voysey, his identity resides in the mere possession of his wealth rather than its use. Even though he has been swindled out of roughly half of his capital he will suffer no diminution of his creature comforts for the rest of his life. Yet both he and Colpus, another client, when they discover the fraud, devise a scheme to avoid bringing in the law and exposing the Voyseys. In effect they blackmail Edward Voysey. They are willing to compound the felony by keeping quiet so long as he makes reparation to them before any other client to the tune of a thousand a year. Their ethics and motives require no comment, but their dishonesty, whilst it compares unfavourably with Voysey's, is just as much a logical result of Barker's depiction of economic reality. The fact that Colpus is the local vicar is an ironic reminder of the ramifications of the nexus of inherited and invested wealth.

The tendentious structuring of the work of Jones, Pinero, and Galsworthy roots their chosen social and moral problems firmly in the dramatic centre of their plays. *The Voysey Inheritance* is remarkable in that much of the play is taken up with day-to-day concerns of Voysey family life which bear no direct connection to the criminality of the family firm. Voysey compartmentalizes his life. He advises Edward: 'You must realise that money making is one thing, and religion another, and family-life a third' (Act 2). Like Wemmick in *Great Expectations*, Voysey specifically advocates a split between business and private life, 'You must learn whatever the business may be to leave it behind you at the Office. Why, life's not worth living else' (Act 1). Barker's presentation of the concerns of the Voysey family represents more than the practical achievement of Voysey's philosophy. It is central to the critique of economic and social formations. When Edward learns of the firm's deceit he is greatly shocked; Voysey comforts him:

'You'll find the household as if nothing had happened. Then you'll remember that nothing really has happened' (Act 1). The trivia of English bourgeois life carries on no matter how shaky its foundations; its stolid respectability depends upon a deceit inherent in its economic base. Moreover, it is the maintenance of unexceptional, even dull, family life which inspires the trust and confidence of Voysey's clients. The result is that he can cheat them with impunity.

Although Barker's commentary on this aspect of the economic system by necessity concerns itself primarily with upper-middle-class life, the organization of the play prevents it from being solely a critical examination of the mores of one particular class. The following stage directions describe Peacey, head clerk of the firm of Voysey and Son:

> *A very drunken client might mistake him for his master. His voice very easily became a toneless echo of Mr Voysey's; later his features caught a line or two from that mirror of all the necessary virtues into which he was so constantly gazing; but how his clothes even when new contrive to look like old ones of Mr Voysey's is a mystery, and to his tailor a most annoying one.* (Act 1)

In the defining system of the play, Peacey's less than successful aping of his employer stresses that his function in Voysey's business is more than that of just employee. As generations of Peaceys succeed each other they blackmail Voysey for their silence. Peacey's hush money amounts to a modest two hundred a year, but his involvement is complete. He is, like George Booth, a parasite on the capitalist system, metaphorically willing to let others do the stealing for him. Unlike Galsworthy, who defined his plays by a vertical section through a hierarchy of separated social classes, Barker's definition is less crude and indicates a more comprehensive and subtle correlation of social classes within the dominant social and economic order. At one point Edward asks his father, 'Is every single person who trusts you involved in your system? . . . My mind travelled naturally from George Booth with his big income to old Nursie with her savings which she brought you to invest' (Act 2). Whether it is Booth with his thousands or Nursie with her five hundred pounds life savings, they both participate and are implicated in Barker's depiction of society's economic base.

Voysey dies between Acts Two and Three. Edward inherits the family firm and its deceit just as Voysey had inherited them from his father. The inheritance of the title of the play is most obviously the bequest of the firm. The financial connotations of inheritance are reinforced by Peacey's two hundred a year which is a bequest from his father when he worked for the firm. But there are more far-reaching associations with the conventions of literary natura-lism. The intimation of a genetic determinant in itself implies that the deceit has a more common typicality than individual roguery and is beyond simple ethical judgements. The other Voysey sons, in spite of, and indeed because of, their superficially impeccable respectability, have little hesitation in advising Edward to con-tinue his father's practice. They implicate a range of Edwardian social and ideological structures: Trenchard, the law; Booth's excessive concern for family honour; and Hugh, the detachment of artistic idealism. Edward's response iterates the implications of naturalist theory: 'Oh, listen to this! First Trenchard . . . and now you! You've the poison in your blood, every one of you. Who am I to talk? I daresay so have I' (Act 3). *The Voysey Inheritance* owes more to Ibsen than Barker's other plays, but the poison in the Voyseys' blood is not, as it is with Oswald in *Ghosts*, literal. The Voysey inheritance is more environmental than hereditary. The Voyseys are the product of internal and external psychological pressures generated by the social and economic formations of Edwardian Britain.

History repeats itself as Edward succeeds his father. Voysey, after his inheritance, manages to rectify the firm's affairs but returns to his father's ways. The motivation is more complex and more subtle than the fact that 'the fascination of swindling one's clients will ultimately prove irresistible' (Act 4). Edward senses a more fundamental latency within himself:

He [Voysey] must have begun like this. Trying to do the right thing in the wrong way . . . then doing the wrong thing . . . then bringing himself to what he was . . . and so me to this. (*He flings away from her*.) No, Alice, I won't do it. I daren't take that first step down. There's a worse risk than any failure. Think . . . I might succeed. (Act 3)

As soon as Edward attempts to do the right thing in the wrong way by putting straight the accounts of the small investors who would be hurt most by a crash, he is enmeshed in the ineluctable psychology of the Voysey system. This is not individual criminality but the inevitable correlative of living within a society whose economic basis is inherited and invested wealth. Alice Maitland, who becomes Edward's fiancée at the end of the play, is a key figure in Barker's inversion of conventional ethical positions. Edward's earlier principles, which involved his acceptance of the legal code as definer of correct and incorrect behaviour, made him a weak, unassertive character. The shouldering of the burden he inherited from his father, the activity of work, and the responsibility of creating one's own ethical standards, define his masculinity. Alice tells Edward, 'There was never any chance of my marrying you when you were only a well-principled prig. I didn't want you . . . and I don't believe you really wanted me. Now you do. And you must always take what you want' (Act 5). She adds sexuality to the comprehensive network of insinuations which makes up the Voysey inheritance.

Aspects of the plotting of *Waste* (1907) – an initial sexual indiscretion, its discovery, and the consequent disgrace of a figure eminent in social and public life followed by his suicide – bear an obvious similarity to the structuring of the well-made society drama. The resemblance is only superficial. Barker's treatment of the material was sufficiently distant from the acceptable gentlemanly launderings of the commercial drama to incite the wrath of the Lord Chamberlain's Office, and the play was banned by the censor, ostensibly because of the frankness of its treatment of sexual relations and its references to an abortion, then a criminal operation. However, it is more likely that the real reason for the ban was because of the play's unsympathetic representation of politicians and its indictment of political life. It did not escape attention at the time that the reference to abortion in Elizabeth Robins' *Votes for Women* did not prevent that play from receiving a licence earlier in the same year.

The difference between *Waste* and the society drama lies only partly in Barker's treatment of illicit sexual relations between Henry Trebell and Amy O'Connell. More radically, the play refutes the validity of those dominant social and ethical codes which control relations between the sexes and whose function as a system of validation lies at the ideological centre of the society drama.

Trebell is a politician and fits therefore into the same sort of social circles presented in the work of Jones and Pinero. However, the fashionable professional man in their drama is defined predominantly by his social position rather than by his actual profession. Similarly, the consequences of irregular sexual relationships are essentially of social concern. In *Waste*, on the other hand, there is a more considerable mediation of Trebell's professional life. This arises not just from incidental and circumstantial detail, though that is there, but because his work, rather than his social position, is the play's dominant defining principle. *Waste* is organized around a set of complex and subtle metaphorical interconnections between Trebell's public and private lives.

Trebell is preparing to steer through parliament a bill to disestablish the Church and, with its money, endow education. For Trebell, as opposed to the party politicians (he was previously unaligned, but has joined forces with the Tories for the purposes of the bill), it is neither merely a piece of legislation nor a stepping-stone in his career; the twin themes of education and faith raise it to the level of a vocation, and in the terms of the play it is an affirmation of life. The concept of 'teaching our children' subsumes the spiritual potency of the Church Trebell plans to disestablish: 'What a Church could be made of the best brains in England, sworn only to learn all they could, teach what they knew, without fear of the future or favour to the past . . . sworn upon their honour as seekers after truth, knowingly to tell no child a lie. It will come' (Act 2). Trebell is no impractical idealist; he operates in a world of the actualities of party politics and powerful lobbies, and it is a world he understands and can manipulate. The conjunction of the power of the visionary and his unquestionable practical ability makes him the most effective and able politician in the play. He delights in manipulation, delights in his consciousness of the power he has to move less aware and more unwitting pieces on the political chessboard:

TREBELL: I'll buy the Church, not with money, but with the promise of new life. (*A certain rather gleeful cunning comes over him.*) It'll only look like a dose of reaction at first . . . Sectarian Training Colleges endowed to the hilt.
WEDGECROFT: What'll the Nonconformists say?
TREBELL: Bribe them with the means of equal efficiency. (Act 2)

In the first act, set on the last evening of a weekend house party, the temper of political life manifests itself in the social tone of the party which is peopled mainly by influential and fashionable politicians, their wives and relatives. They are witty and sophisticated, intelligent and ironic. But there is also an ambience of smugness and self-satisfaction that categorizes a ruling oligarchy which decides important political issues in the same tone as its members chat about golf and billiards. The prelude to the political intrigue depicted in the play is literally by Chopin; Mrs Farrant plays for her guests as the curtain rises and they chat dispassionately about the levels of relative maturity required for the appreciation of Bach and Chopin. The intrigue ends in the penultimate act when senior politicians meet and decide to exclude Trebell from the cabinet; as they leave, the topic of conversation is of a dotty aunt, whom we never see, and her bizarre decision to sell a Holbein. The play's structure contains serious political matters within the trivialities of polite society. In contrast, Trebell's dedication and fervour seem laudable.

His control and dominance in political affairs, however, expresses itself in his seduction of Amy O'Connell. He enjoys the power he establishes over her as he manipulates her into bed, just as he enjoys the intrigues of engineering his bill on to the statute books. He is cold, hard, calculating. His seduction is more logical than sensual. The qualities which seem admirable in the politician are not so in the intimacy of sexual relations. Stripped of ameliorating factors such as love, respect, or friendship, his behaviour towards Mrs O'Connell comes across as arrogant, offensive, and, at times, callous. The starkness of the tone of the relationship is very different from the aura of romance which attaches itself to irregular sexual relationships in the society drama.

Just as Voysey compartmentalizes his life, Trebell attempts to maintain a division between his public world of political affairs and his private world of sexual affairs. Amy O'Connell is a suitable candidate for his attentions as she has little connection with political life. Although present at the house party in the first act, she is noticeably excluded from the political chatter indulged in by the other guests. Not only does she lack the knowledge which would give her access to the range of shared reference enjoyed by the others, she is not interested in acquiring it. Time Trebell spends with Amy is time he can snatch from what he considers more pressing political business. Her interview with him in the second act, when she tells him of her pregnancy, assumes a symbolic significance in the structure of the act: it is squeezed in between two political interviews which Trebell holds; he is 'too busy for love-making now'.

Despite Trebell's belief in a divorce between the two parts of his life, the similarity between his treatment of Amy and his conduct as a politician indicates that there is a fundamental link between the two. In becoming an effective and successful politician Trebell has excluded from his life a full range of emotional responses; he has deliberately failed to realize and has wasted one part of his life. Initially he cherishes the belief that this is his strength. He boasts of his pulse, 'I promise you it hasn't varied a beat these three big months' (Act 2). His arrogance is mistaken and its implications are suggested in an exchange between Mrs Farrant and Lady Davenport earlier in the play:

MRS FARRANT: (*Brilliantly*) I think a statesman may be a little inhuman.

LADY DAVENPORT: (*With keenness*) Do you mean superhuman? It's not the same thing, you know. (Act 1 Scene 1)

Trebell only realizes the deprivation caused by his exaltation of the cold logic of his conduct in political affairs late in the play, after Amy O'Connell and what he considers to be the unborn child have died at the hands of the back-street abortionist and he has been excluded from the cabinet:

TREBELL: . . . I want to think. I haven't thought for years.
FRANCES: Why, you have done nothing else.
TREBELL: I've been working out problems in legal and political algebra. (Act 4 Scene 1)

The killing of the unborn child, as the abortion is seen in the play, is for Trebell the symbolic conjunction of the political and the private. It is a refutation of his political vision translated into concrete personal terms. Amy kills the very thing for which he was to build his scheme of endowed education. Her fear of life, which drives her to the abortionist, is the abnegation of the creativity and affirmation of life which are supposedly immanent in his scheme. Trebell's perception of his scheme encompasses what are for him the fundamental facts of human existence and emotion: 'There are three facts in life that call up emotion . . . Birth, Death, and the Desire for Children. The niceties are shams' (Act 1 Scene 2). But this statement of belief is in essence couched in terms of a political rhetoric. The three facts are abstract, removed from the area of everyday human emotion which they imply and for which Trebell himself makes a claim. He is indifferent to the actual fact of the birth of a child to his cousin, and, on learning of Amy O'Connell's pregnancy, his attitude towards her and the coming child is unemotional and purely practical. Amy's pregnancy is just another problem to be solved. It is only with the death of what would have been *his* child that the truth of his political vision is brought home to him in the emotional terms he has asserted earlier in the play. Amy herself is of no account. It is only because of her pregnancy that she has 'become a person of some importance to the world' (Act 2). Her death is unimportant; it is, Trebell claims, 'a waste of time' (Act 3) even to think of her. As in his education scheme, it is the child alone that counts for anything: 'The little fool, the little fool . . . why did she kill my child? What did it matter what I thought of her? We were committed together to that one thing' (Act 4 Scene 2). This is how the issue is mediated by the symbolic structure of the play; Barker does not recognize it as a construct of male egotism. Although Barker presents Trebell as a flawed character, he nevertheless still expects an audience to identify with his view that the producing of children is necessarily an act of creation. The ideological problematic of the system of validation in *The Marrying of Ann Leete* is here more sharply brought into focus. If Ann is approbated on account of her potential for procreation, the obverse of that system is that Amy is disapprobated by her refusal to have a child. Barker denies women the propriety of their own fertility. The same is also true when Shaw, a more radical socialist, develops his theory of the Life Force.

The possibility of a scandal which inevitably attaches itself to Trebell's transgression of conventional morality takes up most of the third act. But, whilst such material is important as a depiction of the ideological code to which the social class of Trebell's peers subscribe and is therefore necessary to the play's realistic framework, Barker does not employ the relationship between Trebell's behaviour and social and moral codes as the major principle of dramatic definition. This constitutes his departure from the society drama, where the endorsement of the dominant ideology provided the dramatic definition, and also his departure from the work of a dramatist such as Galsworthy, where a criticism of aspects of dominant ideological codes defined the drama. The threat of scandal does not materially affect the plot of the play. Trebell is finally excluded from the cabinet because of political infighting, not because he is genuinely considered to be unfit on account of his moral lapse, nor because the politicians believe that they cannot control the scandal. Barker's reliance on a symbolic network as the primary ordering principle subordinates the definition which inheres in the realistic social setting of the play. In the last act, the central focus is not so much on the public outcome,

Trebell's exclusion from the cabinet, as on his personal realization of the implications of Amy O'Connell's death. The definition arises from the creation of symbolic interconnections between the public and the private – Trebell's work as a politician and Amy O'Connell's pregnancy and death.

Despite Barker's validation of women by their potential or otherwise for procreation, *The Marrying of Ann Leete*, *The Voysey Inheritance*, and *Waste* incidentally touch on how social, economic, and cultural formations impinge on the opportunity of middle-class women to achieve fulfilment and self-determination. *The Madras House* (1910) is his most extensive exploration of the position of women in society. Its structure departs from the dominant mode of Edwardian drama in that it depends not upon a developed plot but a series of loosely connected vignettes which each examine different aspects of the oppression of women. The vignettes are linked by the presence in each of them of Philip Madras who functions more as a sensitive commentator than a participant.

The first act is set in the comfortable middle-class home of Henry Huxtable, wealthy owner of the drapery business Roberts and Huxtable. The house is inhabited by his six unmarried daughters, who are aged between twenty-six and thirty-nine. In the extensive stage directions the plight of Emma, the second youngest daughter, is spelt out: '*She would have been a success in an office and worth perhaps thirty shillings a week. But the* HUXTABLES *don't want another thirty shillings a week and this gift, such as it is, has been wasted, so that* EMMA *runs also to a brusque temper*' (Act 1). Barker's creation of an active principle of definition from an unsensational financial situation is rare in the Edwardian drama of middle-class life. But what Barker does not make clear is that a wage of that sort would imply a considerably lower social position than that actually enjoyed by the Huxtables and would represent an unacceptable loss of caste. The daughters are denied economic independence, but more importantly they are denied access to economic activity. As a result they atrophy. Though the women in *The Liars* and *The Case of Rebellious Susan* may be idle and aimless, their experience and financial standing are a very different affair. The very economic mediocrity of the Huxtables' economic position saps the daughters' enthusiasm and vitality; they have enough money not to make them need to strive for more, but not enough to make them extravagant: 'Father seems afraid of spending money, though he must have got lots. He says if he gave us any more we shouldn't know what to do with it . . . and of course that's true' (Act 1). Gender and class-determined notions of gentility further deprive the daughters of identity and purpose. Emma describes how they fill their lives with activity which is socially acceptable and lady-like but meaningless and trivial: 'We're always busy. I mean there's lots to be done about the house and there's calling and classes and things. Julia used to sketch quite well' (Act 1). Julia's talent resulted in her being sent to art school. Instead of promoting an opportunity for self-validation, her experience merely makes her more unhappy and dissatisfied. She learns only that her talent is mediocre. Barker could have made a more telling point if he had stressed the role the art schools played in offering a way out for middle-class young women. He registers her discontent but could have made it more poignant by showing that having been given the freedom of the art school it is denied her on her return to the family home.

Nevertheless, Barker's depiction of the daughters' experience is an indictment of the formations of bourgeois life. The formations not only oppress but socialize the daughters so that they are unable properly to analyse or conceive of ways of changing their position. Their conversation largely comprises of phatic communion; its trivia – polite formalities of introduction and leave-taking, remarks about the weather and the view from the window – is rendered even more inane by its perpetual repetition. The repetition makes its very banality comic; as Gerald Weales comments, 'Only a saving irony keeps Act One of *The Madras House* from being as boring to the reader as it is to the characters' (p. 185). More than a technique of dramatic writing which creates the impression of real speech patterns, the tedium of the dialogue is an effective mediation of the daughters' experience.

The thematic link between the Huxtable girls and the rest of the play lies in the repression of their sexuality. Of the daughters only Jane, the youngest, has had an offer of marriage, but the dictates of middle-class nicety put a stop to it because 'they heard of something he'd once done' (Act 1). The formations of middle-class family life deem that marriage is the only structure which would provide them with appropriate employment and sexual experience. But they seem doomed to spinsterhood and therefore celibacy. Their psychological distortion is succinctly adumbrated in one incident:

> A collar marked Lewis Waller came back from the wash in mistake for one of father's. I don't think he lives near here, but it's one of those big steam laundries. And Morgan the cook got it and she gave it to Julia . . . and Julia kept it. And when mother found out she cried for a whole day. She said it showed a wanton mind. (Act 1)

Barker here makes reference to a real person and he could confidently expect that its significance would have been known to his audience. Lewis Waller was an extremely popular star of the Edwardian stage, his fans wore badges emblazoned with the letters KOW indicating that they were 'Keen on Waller'. Julia's fantasizing over a contemporary stage idol is adolescent – but Julia is thirty-four.

The second act is set in the business offices of Roberts and Huxtable. The living-in system of Huxtable's drapery establishment is as oppressive as the middle-class home, and economics just as crucial. For the consideration of the notional element of thirty pounds a year for living out, Brigstock, 'Third Man in the Hosiery', lives in. Consequently he is forced to keep his marriage a secret and for four years has lived apart from his wife. Brigstock, seduced by the capitalist myth, endures this self-imposed separation in order to raise enough money to start his own business. But despite the economies he makes by living in, his dream is probably as futile as Julia's of Lewis Waller. However, as in the first act, it is women who suffer most. Mrs Brigstock can only just keep her hysteria under control: 'I lie awake at night away from him till I could scream with thinking about it. And I do scream as loud as I dare . . . not to wake the house. And if somebody don't open that window, I shall go off' (Act 2).

If the first act shows how the middle-class Huxtable daughters are condemned to meaningless domesticity, the second act examines a structure which does allow economic independence for women. Nevertheless, the living-in system becomes a metaphor for the oppression and control of women's lives and sexuality in ways which economic independence alone cannot challenge. Miss Chancellor, the living-in housekeeper, is the agent of that control. She endeavours to use it to influence the girls in her charge 'towards the virtues of modesty and decorum' (Act 2). In effect the system imposes on working women, despite their economic independence, those social and moral codes which deny any expression of female sexuality outside the one approbated structure of marriage. This is of course just one strategy in a more pervasive and extensive system of control. In the terms of the play, Miss Chancellor is also a victim of the system she administers. She is a spinster and implicitly this is a correlative of her own economic independence. Although she exalts her independence from and indifference to men, this seems largely an apology for her personal position, and her stern moralism seems a function of her sexual deprivation. Huxtable, despite his general kindliness and good intentions, is the keeper of a domestic and industrial seraglio.

Marion Yates, a shop assistant, is like Miss Chancellor also unmarried. She is in this implicitly another product of the living-in system. But she is pregnant. Although others in the play see this as moral and social deviation, she has symbolically as well as literally evaded Miss Chancellor's policing. She refuses to reveal the father of her child (it turns out to be Constantine Madras) and by refusing to consider marriage she rejects structures of male authority and concepts of social and moral reparation for her immodest behaviour. She is of course a key figure and is validated as much by her pregnancy as by her challenge to dominant codes. The stage directions which describe her indicate Barker's approval: '*To the seeing eye she glows in that room like a live coal. She has genius – she has life*' (Act 2).

The link between the first two acts lies in their thematic consistency. The third act, set in the fashion house of the title, extends the implications of these themes and abandons the naturalistic definition of Huxtable's daughters and employees for a more metaphorical examination of the construction of gender and sexuality. The orientalism of the decor with its Moorish rotunda, Persian carpet and crescent shaped light fittings, underscores the suggestions of imperial exploitation contained in the play's title which provides an analogue for its main concern – the exploitation of women. The orientalism is, though, a sham and, as Barker comments in the stage directions, '*it is all about as Moorish as Baker Street Station*'. In contrast to the domestic realism of the first two acts, the action now takes on the air of grotesque fantasy. This is emphasized by the apparition of a mannequin parade. The manager who directs the parade is a neutered functionary of the fashions he places on display. The models themselves, literally the objects of gaze, are the most obvious metaphor for the objectification of female sexuality. They have no identity apart from the fashions they parade and the numbers they are allotted. The titillation they and their fashions provoke is nervous and artificial, for the mannequins themselves are in fact dehumanized. The element of the ludicrous in the plan to replace them with mechanical moving figures is subsumed by the symbolic appropriateness of the suggestion.

The exploitation of women and the appropriation of their sexuality is metaphorically restated in images of prostitution. Parisian fashions, designed for the respectable middle classes, follow those of the French cocotte, la Belle Hélène; as Philip Madras wryly observes, 'What can be more natural and right than for the professional charmer to set the pace for the amateur' (Act 3). And Eustace Perrin State, who is in negotiation to buy the Madras House, has a Nottingham retail outlet where the 'Ladies' department [is] served by gentlemen . . . the Gentlemen's by ladies'. The undercurrent of salaciousness in his description is barely disguised by the claim that 'anything Depraved' is rigorously avoided.

State is a caricature of the American businessman. His methods and ideas place the keystone on the exploitation of women by commercial culture. Middle-class women, for him, merely constitute 'one of the greatest Money Spending Machines the world has ever seen' (Act 3). Similarly the prospect of the women's movement brings out the visionary in him. But his vision is that it will not result in liberation and self-determination, but in women expressing themselves by buying the fashions *he* is going to provide for them. He will construct their sexuality. Although State is satirically undermined by the urbane irony of Philip and Constantine Madras, he represents a new era in commerce and retailing. The scientific principles of market research, which he advocates, make the onward march of a crass and constricting commercial culture seem inevitable. If so, women's economic power will merely further enmesh them in their oppression. Barker's vision is bleak, but he has a comprehensive grasp of the real power of oppressive structures to assimilate and draw the teeth of opposition.

With the exception of Marion Yates's pregnancy, any positions which challenge the dominant structures of relations between the sexes are inadequate. Constantine Madras's embracing of the Islamic faith appears at first to be such a challenge. But in the last act his hypocrisy is revealed. His choice of religion is merely a convenient endorsement of his polygamous predilections and his sexual chauvinism. *The Madras House*, instead of a denouement, ends with a protracted discussion between Philip Madras and his wife. They talk of the nature of their own relationship and touch on many of the play's themes. Although Philip is throughout the play the most perceptive commentator on society's structures, he also is their victim. His dichotomy is the dichotomy of the play. The subtlety of his intellect enables him to analyse the problems but it is also a product of cultural forces and therefore makes any enacting of solutions almost as difficult for him as it is for the Huxtable daughters. His decision not to accept a position in State's commercial empire may salve his own conscience but it won't stop State; on a personal level maybe he and his wife will be able to re-negotiate their relationship but it won't affect institutional structures. At the end there is optimism but no real resolution.

The play breaks off mid-sentence, and the final stage direction reads, '*She doesn't finish, for really there is no end to the subject*'. Perhaps Philip's decision to go on the County Council is the right decision; reform of the structures which oppress women is a political issue.

Of Barker's plays *The Madras House* dispenses the most comprehensively with conventional plotting strategies. Incidents within the play – the question of the paternity of Miss Yates's child, the sale of the Madras House, the strained relations between Philip and his wife, or the estrangement between Constantine Madras and his – are all material which is susceptible to mediation via the techniques of the conventional well-made play, but here they are no more than incidents. Barker avoids the concatenation of plotting strategy and ideological statement which characterizes the work of Jones, Pinero, and Galsworthy. His play is ordered not by plot but by its thematic unity mediated through a system of interconnecting metaphors. Even the more conventionally plotted *Waste* and *The Voysey Inheritance* are not resolved by their plots. Trebell's suicide, unlike Paula Tanqueray's, is not a convenient solution of an awkward social problem nor is it a gesture of despair. It refuses to avail itself of conventional attitudes, and Trebell's motivation is left nebulous and tentative, his death an open-ended statement. Similarly, at the end of *The Voysey Inheritance* there is no certainty as to whether George Booth will decide to expose the fraud nor a clear indication of how Edward will administer the Voysey inheritance. Edward and Alice's decision to marry suggests departure not closure. Again the subordination of elements of plot emphasizes the metaphorical implications of the plays.

For the original audiences this made Barker's work less accessible than that of Jones, Pinero, and Galsworthy. Even supporters of the new drama were often mystified. He was ahead of his time as well as part of it. His understanding of the structures and codes of Edwardian society was more subtle than that of those dramatists, and he developed techniques which mediated more effectively the complexities and contradictions of those structures and codes.

V
Shaw

George Bernard Shaw was born in 1856 in Dublin into a middle-class protestant family. His father owned a wholesale cornmilling business which provided a modest but precarious living. His mother was a talented amateur musician and singer. After his formal education at lower-middle-class catholic and protestant schools ended at the age of fifteen, his uncle's influence secured a position for Shaw as a junior clerk in a prestigious Dublin firm of land agents and after a year or so he was promoted to cashier. He resigned the post in 1876 and went to London, following his mother who had left her husband and taken her daughters there in 1873.

Apart from brief employment with the Edison Telephone Company of London, the move to England marks the beginnings of Shaw's literary career. In 1879 he completed his first novel *Immaturity*, and by 1883 had written four more: *The Irrational Knot*, *Love among the Artists*, *Cashel Byron's Profession*, and *An Unsocial Socialist*. Four of them received serial publication between 1884 and 1888. Throughout the latter part of the 1880s and most of the 1890s Shaw was a prolific reviewer. He was book critic for the *Pall Mall Gazette*, art critic for *The World*, music critic for *The Star* and later *The World*, and most importantly for his later career, between 1895 and 1898 drama critic for the *Saturday Review*. Probably the other single most important event during this period was his joining the Fabian Society in 1884.

In 1885, in collaboration with William Archer, he began the play that in 1892 would be staged by the Independent Theatre Society as *Widowers' Houses*. Shaw, with a characteristic amount of mannered self-dramatization and ironic self-conceit, described the circumstances surrounding its production in the Preface to *Plays Unpleasant*:

> [The Independent Theatre] got on its feet by producing Ibsen's Ghosts; but its search for unacted native dramatic masterpieces was so complete a failure that in the autumn of 1892 it had not yet produced a single original piece of any magnitude by an English author. In this humiliating national emergency, I proposed to Mr Grein that he should boldly announce a play by me. Being an extraordinarily sanguine and enterprising man, he took this step without hesitation. I then raked out, from my dustiest pile of discarded and rejected manuscripts, two acts of a play I had begun in 1885 . . . in collaboration with my friend William Archer. (*B H S*, I, p.17)

The tone and the polemical strategy are commonplaces of Shaw's discursive writing. That they should appear in a preface to the published edition of the plays creates the experience, unique in Edwardian drama, of the Shaw play. The prefatory and, on occasion, postscriptural material is simultaneously external to the plays proper, and integral to our experience of them. The experience of reading the published volume of, for example, *Man and Superman* where the play is sandwiched between the 'Epistle Dedicatory' to A. B. Walkley and 'The Revolutionist's Handbook and Pocket Companion' purportedly by John Tanner (which itself is sandwiched between its own foreword and a collection of 'Maxims for Revolutionists') is a vastly different affair from experiencing *Man and Superman* in the theatre. Indeed, as the long dream sequence of Don Juan in Hell, which is interpolated into the third act of what would otherwise be a superficially conventional four-act romantic comedy, is often omitted in production, the experience of reading the play on its own can be different from the theatrical experience of *Man and Superman*. The disparity between the experiences, as in most of Shaw's plays, is compounded by the interspersal throughout the text of lengthy passages of explicit analysis and commentary printed as stage directions. These may be valuable indirect pointers for actors and directors but have little direct tangible existence in the theatre. This is not to imply that the plays are flawed because they depend upon extra-theatrical (or what the hostile commentator calls novelistic) apparatus but to acknowledge the results of the literary mode of production of Shaw's plays.

Copyright legislation at the end of the 1880s placed a legal restraint on the blatant piracy of dramatists' work which had been common earlier in the century. From the beginning of the 1890s, the prestige and protection the legislation afforded dramatists was apparent in the vastly improved published editions of plays aimed at an audience of play readers. Shaw's uniqueness lies in the extent to which he exploited the opportunities brought about by developments in the dissemination of play texts in the late Victorian period. Throughout the nineteenth century, acting editions of plays in flimsy paper covers had been issued by firms such as Lacy, Dicks, and French, but from the early 1890s commercial dramatists such as Jones and Pinero published high quality hardback editions of their plays, in which the technical stage directions of the acting editions were replaced by lengthier, more general ones clearly provided for a reader's not the theatre's convenience. Most of Pinero's printed plays are prefaced by a note 'Throughout, "Right" and "Left" are the spectator's Right and Left, not the actor's'. The directions in Jones's and Pinero's work are admittedly of a different order from those of Shaw, but the element of extended analysis and ironic commentary in the directions of other late Victorian and Edwardian dramatists such as Harley Granville Barker and J. M. Barrie serve precisely the same function in terms of the literary mode of production of the drama.

Even so, Shaw's published work differs in two crucial respects. Whereas the publication of most play texts succeeded or was aimed to coincide with stage production, the publication of Shaw's plays often preceded performance in the full knowledge that production by commercial managements was highly unlikely and production by minority theatre ventures by no means certain. Secondly, most plays were initially published as single volumes. In Shaw's case, the collation of several plays and extensive retrospective prefaces into single volumes with titles like *Plays Unpleasant*, *Plays Pleasant*, *Three Plays for Puritans* lends his work a programmatic appearance both as individual plays and as collections.

Plays Unpleasant announces its firm allegiance to the independent theatre movement and what was seen as the school of Ibsen in direct confrontation with the anodyne entertainment values of the commercial stage. In tackling subjects such as slum landlordism and prostitution Shaw was unbandaging the open sores and throwing open the doors and windows of the lazar house. Shaw places his work within what, from a modern standpoint, is an identifiable tradition of nineteenth-century theatre. The 'pleasant' and 'puritanical' plays are identifiable in other nineteenth-century traditions more conventionally associated with the commercial stage: *The Devil's Disciple* (1907) with melodrama as practised at the Adelphi; *Caesar and Cleopatra* (1907) with large scale historical spectacle drama; *Candida* (1900) with domestic drama; *Arms and the Man* (1894) with romantic comedy and military melodrama; *You Never Can Tell* (1899) with farcical comedy. Shaw is, of course, manipulating the conventions of these genres for his own ends. Galsworthy, for instance, by employing the emotional strategies of domestic melodrama to reinforce his ideological bias, subsumed the conventions of melodrama as part of the recreation of actuality upon which his drama purports to be founded. Shaw's engagement with the traditions of nineteenth-century theatre was made in order to expose its conventions as arrant romantic and sentimental nonsense. More than a parody of theatrical convention, Shaw offers a critique of the ethical and ideological assumptions of the drama, and, by extension, he exposes the mythologized versions of those theatrical assumptions which inhere in the social and ideological formations of real life.

Inversely, Shaw's manipulation of familiar convention and formulas became a means to woo commercial managements. Unlike other minority dramatists, he envisaged his work as a provocative challenge to be accepted by the stars and actor managers of the Edwardian stage. Even in *The Philanderer* (1907), avowedly billed as an 'unpleasant' play, he claimed, 'I had written a part which nobody but Charles Wyndham could act, in a play which was impossible at his theatre' (*B H S*, I, p. 19). Later, *Captain Brassbound's Conversion* (1900) was written with Ellen

Terry in mind, *Caesar and Cleopatra* for Forbes Robertson and Mrs Patrick Campbell, *The Devil's Disciple* for William Terriss, *The Man of Destiny* (1901) for Henry Irving, and in 1897 the germ of an idea for a play which was later to become *Pygmalion* (1914) was conceived as a vehicle for Forbes Robertson and Mrs Patrick Campbell. (The parts of Henry Higgins and Eliza Doolittle were eventually created by Beerbohm Tree and Mrs Patrick Campbell.) In the second decade of the twentieth century some of Shaw's plays were being accepted by commercial managements, but as the decade progressed many of the grand figures of the 1890s, whom Shaw had provoked, had disappeared from the stage and he had already written the bulk of his significant work.

Widowers' Houses opens as if it is to proceed as a conventional romantic comedy. The Rhineland setting, the gentle satire of the English abroad fully equipped with the holy writ of Baedekers and continental Bradshaws, the incipient romance between Trench and Blanche Sartorius, his tongue-tied wooing and, at this stage at least, her more forceful encouragement, all fit a familiar pattern. The drama seems as if it will resolve itself into a comedy in which the problems of misalliance provide obstacles to the lovers to be overcome by their eventual match by the end of the play. The misalliance theme is inverted by Shaw. The initial obstacle does not arise from the expectation that Trench's aristocratic relations will oppose the marriage to Blanche, but from Sartorius. He demands that Trench produce written evidence that Trench's family will accept on terms of total equality the daughter of a man who is aggressively unashamed of the fact that his considerable wealth was self-made. But in the second act Shaw subverts expectations he has set up in the first.

The obstacle comes not from Trench's family, nor from Sartorius. Trench himself objects when he discovers that the source of Sartorius's income is from the rack-renting of slum property. Although Shaw's attitude towards Ireland was ambiguous, his Irishness and his knowledge of Irish history added a particular trenchancy to his perception of the relationship between landlord and tenant. The elder Malone in *Man and Superman* does not forget the history of his own land: 'Me father died of starvation in

Ireland in the black 47 . . . Me father was starved dead; and I was starved out to America in me mother's arms. English rule drove me and mine out of Ireland' (Act 4). Nevertheless, in terms of Shaw's modulation of the conventions of nineteenth-century drama, he draws on a set of emotional and ethical structures which were at least sixty years old. Sartorius is now cast in the role of wicked foreclosing landlord, and Lickcheese, the rent collector, as that of his bullying agent. Trench learns the truth from Lickcheese who has just been dismissed for spending twenty-four shillings on repairs: 'Look at that bag of money on the table. Hardly a penny of that but there was a hungry child crying for the bread it would have bought' (Act 2). The intonation of *Widowers' Houses* has shifted from romantic comedy to domestic melodrama. The indictment of prodigal absentee landlords in Douglas Jerrold's *The Rent-Day* (1832) is directly comparable: 'If the landlord lose at gaming, his tenants must suffer for't. The Squire plays a low card – issue a distress warrant! He throws deuce-ace – turn a family into the fields! 'Tis only awkward to lose hundreds on a card; but very rascally to be behind-hand with one's rent!' (Act 1 Scene 1). In keeping with the endorsed ethical centre of domestic melodrama and with his apparent role as hero, Trench denounces Sartorius for the source of his income and refuses to touch the tainted money. If Blanche and he are to marry, it must be on his income of £700 a year. According to theatrical convention true love is above filthy lucre. But incomes are relative. Whilst Trench's income is meagre in comparison to Sartorius's and would not keep Blanche in the manner to which she is accustomed, it is something in the region of ten times greater than a junior clerk would have earned.

Shaw, however, does not allow Trench the luxury of his high moral tone for long. Blanche, with a keen eye on her creature comforts, views his refusal of her father's money as folly and can only account for it by an underhand attempt on Trench's part to wheedle his way out of the marriage. Although she is ignorant of the source of her father's wealth at this stage in the play, she will, unlike the traditional stage heroine, continue to be pragmatic rather than principled. The most effective rebuff to Trench's position comes from Sartorius himself. He simply refuses to fit the mould of melodramatic villain. He is not motivated by vindictiveness, and proceeds to explain rationally to Trench the economic logic of rented property which constrains his actions no matter what his private feelings may be. His justification lies in his only charging the 'recognized fair London rent', that he is in a sense offering a valuable social service (he simply provides 'homes suited to the small means of very poor people, who require roofs to shelter them just like other people'), and that because 'these poor people do not know how to live in proper dwellings', were he to carry out repairs the timber would merely be chopped up by the tenants for fuel. Sartorius's justifications are not untypical of a certain economic and ideological rationale. The rationale is, of course, fundamentally specious and implicitly dishonest, and members of an audience, if they deny its economic and ideological basis, can easily counter its validity. Whilst bemoaning Trench's lack of political acumen which prevents him from similarly confounding Sartorius's arguments, the audience can still allow themselves the luxury of siding with his ethical stance and the populism of domestic melodrama like *The Rent-Day*.

The strategy of Shaw's next revelation in the play aims to undermine any sense of moral superiority Trench may feel and therefore negate the audience's endorsement of his position. Trench's own income derives from a mortgage on Sartorius's property; the landlord does not spare Trench or the audience from the implications of this:

When I, to use your own words, screw, and bully, and drive these people to pay what they have freely undertaken to pay me, I cannot touch one penny of the money they give me until I have first paid you your seven hundred a year out of it. What Lickcheese did for me, I do for you. He and I are alike intermediaries: you are the principal. It is because of the risks I run through the poverty of my tenants that you exact interest from me at the monstrous and exorbitant rate of seven per cent, forcing me to exact the uttermost farthing in my turn from the tenants. (Act 2)

Trench is unwittingly fully implicated in Sartorius's business. Shaw denies the easy attribution of condemnation or endorsement of individual characters. His analysis is that the structures of capitalism are such that to exist in capitalist society makes it impossible not to collude with Sartorius, and this includes the audience. No one can escape dirtying their hands no matter what comfort can be derived from the luxury of expounding high-minded ethical stances or even oppositional ideological positions.

The play invokes a closed system of definition in which the only ethic is making money. Consequently Trench's idealism turns out to be no more than implicitly hypocritical attitudinizing, and, in comparison to Sartorius's blunt openness and the energy with which he has pursued his business, Trench's passive enjoyment of material benefits from activity he would prefer to condemn makes him, like George Booth and Colpus in *The Voysey Inheritance*, a less admirable character. Trench is *'morally beggared'* by his new-found understanding and rendered incapable of response or action.

In the last act Shaw engineers a situation that forces Trench to make what in the conventional play would be an ethical choice. Lickcheese, sensationally transformed from down-at-heel rent collector to wealthy property speculator in his own right, offers Sartorius the opportunity to participate in a swindle. By dubious means Lickcheese has learnt that Sartorius's property will be compulsorily purchased to make way for a municipal development. If the slum property is improved, a killing is to be made on the compensation. The dishonest scheme requires not only the consent of the ground landlord, Lady Roxdale, but the involvement of the principal mortgagee, her nephew Trench. Trench immediately recognizes the hypocritical sophistry of Sartorius's and Lickcheese's new argument that it is his and their duty to society to put the property into good repair. What Trench intends to be a taunt – 'it appears that the dirtier a place is the more rent you get; and the decenter it is, the more compensation you get. So we're to give up dirt and go in for decency' (Act 3) – is accepted by Sartorius as a frank assessment of the case. Trench's initial response is in keeping with his barely intact moral sensibility.

Even though he has previously argued for the improvement of the property, he will have nothing to do with the swindle posing as the 'philanthropic tack'. But it turns out that this does not constitute the ethical decision Trench has to make. If Trench does not come in with the scheme, Sartorius will buy him out of the profitable mortgage. Trench is faced with the practical consequences of not being linked to Sartorius's business; if his capital is invested in safer and more respectable Consols his income will drop from £700 to £250 a year. Trench's last act in the play is to shake Sartorius's hand and agree to stand in on the scheme. The terms of the economic analysis Shaw offers in *Widowers' Houses* suggest that in a capitalist, and therefore unjust society, it is impossible or folly for a person to attempt to act justly.

Trench is not motivated by economic self-interest alone. Between Sartorius's ultimatum and Trench's decision Shaw returns to a bizarre modulation of the conventions of romantic comedy with which the play opened. Blanche Sartorius, alone with Trench, launches into a virulent attack on him. Shaw underlines the dynamic of the encounter in the stage directions: '*For a moment they stand face to face, quite close to one another, she is provocative, taunting, half defying, half inviting him to advance, in a flush of undisguised animal excitement. It suddenly flashes on him that all this ferocity is erotic: that she is making love to him. His eyes light up: a cunning expression comes into the corners of his mouth*' (Act 3). Just as Alice Maitland cemented Edward Voysey's inheritance, Blanche Sartorius's more explicit and aggressive sexuality defeats whatever conventional principles Trench may have left. Ironically, the young lovers have eventually overcome the obstacles which separated them. Shaw's economic analysis reinterprets the conventions of romantic comedy. Cockayne's pompous remark in the first act that the social trifles of marriage are 'really the springs and wheels of a great aristocratic system' is true, but not in the way that he appears to mean. The aristocratic system is in fact capitalism and that has little to do with class but plenty to do with wealth. Lickcheese's observation that the renting of slum property in Bethnal Green, St Giles's and Marylebone fetches in more per cubic foot than mansions in Park

Lane, indicates that successful capitalist enterprise is no considerer of respectability and class as they are conventionally constituted. The match of Trench and Blanche was never from the start in any way a misalliance. It is a triumphant recognition that the economic activity and interests of the aristocratic family of Lady Roxdale and the family of the self-made rack-renter are identical.

The strategy of *Mrs Warren's Profession* (1902) proceeds along much the same lines as that of *Widowers' Houses*. As Sartorius subverted the stage tradition of the wicked landlord so does Mrs Warren for the tradition of the wicked woman. In the Preface, Shaw claims that he rejects the conventional presentation which the commercial stage employed to make such figures both fascinating and permissible. The conditions are that 'they are beautiful, exquisitely dressed, and sumptuously lodged and fed; also that they shall, at the end of the play, die of consumption to the sympathetic tears of the whole audience, or step into the next room to commit suicide, or at least be turned out by their protectors, and passed on to be "redeemed" by old and faithful lovers' (*B H S*, I, p. 237). Shaw indicts specifically *La Dame aux Camélias* (1852) and *The Second Mrs Tanqueray* in his first two models, and, in his third, the sort of drama represented by Jones's *Saints and Sinners* (1884). Mrs Warren is, however, a rather different sort of figure. She has not been the glamorous kept mistress nor the gullible innocent wickedly seduced but, as the title implies, a professional prostitute. The word profession is not used euphemistically, as it usually is in this context, but literally. Whilst Shaw does reject the commercial drama's plotting strategies which he describes in the preface, his reliance on the semiotic strategy is, as we shall see, far more ambiguous.

Shaw's analysis of the cause of prostitution is economic; it is an inevitable correlative of the exploitation of working-class female labour by the formations of capitalist society. Working-class women are underpaid and overworked; poverty and the conditions of their work wears them out by the age of forty with the only future lying in the workhouse infirmary; certain women's work is responsible for appalling industrial diseases – lead poisoning, phossy jaw, etc. In these circumstances women turn to prostitution simply to survive. Shaw's analysis of the economics and conditions of this sort of women's work denies the validity of dominant ethical codes and the ethical definition in terms of which women's experience is constructed in nineteenth-century drama. Shaw creates a pragmatic ethic which inverts the dominant. A woman has a duty to herself which, given the position of women in society, renders observance of the construct of female respectability a folly and sensibly conducted prostitution a virtue. However, Shaw's presentation of Mrs Warren's experience mediates a significantly different experience.

Shaw establishes a further link between capitalism and prostitution. He demonstrates that the logic and exercise of free enterprise capitalism is no different from that of Mrs Warren's profession. Just as Granville-Barker, in *The Voysey Inheritance*, invokes the logic of capitalism to expose the concept of property as inscribed in the legal code, Shaw does the same for the regulation of sexual behaviour. In an economic system governed by commodity value, Mrs Warren and her sister capitalize on their assets to their own, not others', advantage: 'All we had was our appearance and our turn for pleasing men. Do you think we were such fools as to let other people trade in our good looks by employing us as shopgirls, or bar-maids, or waitresses, when we could trade in them ourselves and get all the profits instead of starvation wages?' (Act 2). At the same time that Shaw, through Mrs Warren, demonstrates that individual prostitutes can justify their activity in terms of the capitalist ethic, through Sir George Crofts, her initial financial backer, he demonstrates that the organization of prostitution in a larger context is, like rackrenting, merely one of the interdependent strands of capitalist investment, return and profit. Those specifically implicated by Crofts include not only the aristocracy (as in *Widowers' Houses*) but the Ecclesiastical Commissioners, Members of Parliament, and England's oldest and most prestigious educational institutions. The Crofts/Warren string of brothels with branches in Brussels, Ostend, Vienna, and Budapest draws off and feeds into the heart of economic activity just like any other international capitalist concern.

Shaw's analysis as a whole begs a great many questions. He runs too much together. He elides distinctions between working-class and middle-class experience and opportunities for women. Mrs Warren herself speaks of factory work, service industry work, and professions such as music, the stage, and journalism, as if they all presented equal access and equal opportunity. One would imagine that Shaw did not share her misguided view. But what is undeniably true is that the play only presents working-class employment opportunities. Shaw ignores the fact that middle-class women did have professions such as teaching, secretarial work, art, opening up to them. Even if we accept his analysis of the relationship of working-class women's work and prostitution, the same is not true for middle-class women. Similarly, Shaw elides different forms of prostitution. Mrs Warren's profession is not just one profession. A middle-class woman could stand a better chance of becoming, like Paula Tanqueray, a wealthy man's kept mistress. Although she technically prostitutes herself, that is not the same thing as working in a brothel. And working in Mrs Warren's high-class brothel is not the same thing as working the streets. And, most importantly, none of these is the same thing as running a brothel.

These failings are concomitant with the way Shaw chooses to present Mrs Warren and are a function of the need to make her an interesting stage character by elevating her status. Even in her early career Mrs Warren never worked in the match factory or the white lead works. Her personal experience has by her own admission been in 'upper'-working-class employment – shop and bar work, waitressing. And in her later career, although *Mrs Warren's Profession* aims to be about prostitution, Shaw presents her less as prostitute, kept mistress, or, ultimately, as brothel owner, than as a member of the managerial class. Implicitly Shaw's play depends upon those theatrical conventions which could most effectively mediate middle-class ways of living.

Shaw's strategy in both *Widowers' Houses* and *Mrs Warren's Profession* is to indict 'defective social organization' (*B H S*, I. p. 34) not the stage figures who administer that organization. His aim was to deny the audience the comfort of evading their own culpability by participating in the comfort of what he described as the 'dramatic illusion of Socialism . . . which presents the working-class as a virtuous hero and heroine in the toils of a villain called "the capitalist" ' (Shaw, 1965, p. 415). He further observed that, when this attitude is transferred to the stage 'the dissentients are treated by the dramatist as enemies to be piously glorified or indignantly vilified' (*B H S*, I, p. 373). But, when the villainous capitalist is Mrs Warren rather than Sartorius, Shaw is implicated rather more than he knows in the conventional treatment of the courtesan on the stage.

Mrs Warren's Profession, despite the rationality of its economic analysis of the causes of prostitution, depends upon the evocation of a covert prurient interest in the protagonist and her employees' activities no less than that provoked by Marguérite Gautier or Paula Tanqueray. Although the play is, in an Edwardian context, remarkably outspoken, Shaw is still extremely coy when it comes to the mediation of Mrs Warren's own experience as prostitute. Despite Shaw's sense of himself as a progressive and advanced dramatist, he suffers in comparison with the novel. Gissing, Moore and Maugham, for instance, were far less circumspect. Mrs Warren's daughter Vivie, hard-headed as she is, is reduced to innuendo which, whilst refusing to be explicit, leaves no doubt as to what she means: 'The two infamous words that describe what my mother is are ringing in my ears and struggling on my tongue; but I can't utter them' (Act 4). More than a social code which prevents a woman uttering the unmentionable, which is Vivie's own explanation, this is characteristic of the play as a whole. This is not to say that Shaw does not convey with some precision the degradation of a prostitute's experience. Mrs Warren herself is explicit: 'Ive often pitied a poor girl, tired out and in low spirits, having to try to please some man that she doesnt care two straws for – some half-drunken fool that thinks he's making himself agreeable when he's teasing and worrying and disgusting a woman so that hardly any money could pay her for putting up with it' (Act 2). Yet what is crucial is that the experience is another's. Throughout the play, in keeping with Mrs Warren's middle-class status, Shaw consistently distances her from the more distasteful aspects of her profession. Her early family and economic circumstances are graphically recounted, but the transition from prostitute to successful entrepreneurial brothel-owner is glossed over. Shaw's treatment is thus tainted by at least some of the sense of mystery and glamour which he indicted in other drama. The differences in the treatment of Sartorius and Mrs Warren are further dependent upon a subscription to dominant gender attributes. Sartorius is indifferent to the plight of those who supply his income; Mrs Warren, despite Shaw's assertion that she 'is much worse than a prostitute' (Shaw, *Collected Letters*, I. p. 566), is caring of her working girls and gratified, as she would be for a daughter, when they do well for themselves.

Similarly, issues are clouded by Shaw's mediation of Mrs Warren's sexuality. Unlike Sartorius, her relation to her business is not purely economic. Her flirtation with Frank suggests that she has a taste for the trade, and Shaw exploits the frisson of a possible sexual encounter between an older experienced woman and a younger, inexperienced man. He may have claimed that he did not deduce her character from her occupation (*B H S*, I, p. 257), but some aspects of her sexuality and conduct are for Shaw, as in more conventional dramas, correlatives of the fallen woman.

The equivalent figure to Trench, set up to posit conventional attitudes in order that the play can then demolish them, is Vivie Warren. She espouses that conventionally moralistic aspect of self-help which urges that one should be content with humble respectability and a modest sufficiency: 'Everybody has some choice, mother. The poorest girl alive may not be able to choose between being Queen of England or Principal of Newnham; but she can choose between ragpicking and flowerselling, according to her taste. People are always blaming their circumstances for what they are' (Act 2). Its validity disintegrates when her mother explains the reality of the circumstances of women's work, and, as a position, it is hopelessly outmatched by the *real ekonomik* of the way in which Crofts and Mrs Warren have helped themselves. Vivie, like Trench, has no effective argument to counter the economic analysis, and, similarly, a reliance on self-righteousness is undercut by her own dependence on the profits of her mother's business. Ironically, the education which enables her economic independence by the end of the play is not only made possible by her dependence on her mother's earnings but on her receipt of the Crofts Scholarship, itself endowed from the profits of the sweated labour which forces women into prostitution.

Vivie's function is more complex than that of Trench as she embodies not only his role but the function of Blanche as well. Sartorius's claim that his involvement in rack-renting is to enable him to provide for his daughter inculpates those constructs of the sanctity of the family and parental/filial devotion which lie at the ethical and ideological centre of domestic melodrama. The relationship between Mrs Warren and her daughter renegotiates these constructs. Mrs Warren is far from being the model mother figure, and Vivie feels none of the usual filial obligations. However, Vivie's attitude undergoes sudden shifts, unlike that of Blanche, whose devotion to her father remains fairly constant. After hearing her mother's account of her early life and entry into prostitution, she experiences a theatrically appropriate gush of daughterly sympathy, respect, and support. The role of dutiful daughter does not last for long; when she discovers that her mother is still involved in financing and managing brothels without the excuse of current economic necessity, Vivie's initial repugnance becomes implacable. This is more than a plot device to lead the audience into the final act. Vivie's behaviour is an enactment of the shallow hypocrisy of the emotional and ideological structures of conventional drama which invite sympathy for the fallen woman at the same time as condemning her.

The resolution of *Mrs Warren's Profession* reverses the uniting of commercial enterprise and matrimony which the match of Blanche and Trench represents. By refusing Crofts' proposal of marriage Vivie declines the cosy option of keeping the business in the family. She rejects all association with her mother including the tainted parental allowance. She is not to be bought for money as her mother has been. The implications of her decision are more complex than a simple inversion of Trench's willing immersion in deceit and fraud. Her education gives her economic independence and entry to a career. She is to be a 'woman of business, permanently single . . . and permanently unromantic' (Act 4). The play asserts the essential importance of education and opportunities for economic independence if women are to escape Mrs Warren's profession. Yet, although Vivie may escape, her position is not without its contradictions. Her chosen career as actuarial statistician fully implicates her as one of the unseen functionaries of capitalism. She may claim that her work is not her mother's work, but the supposed neutrality of double entry book-keeping and profit and loss accounting keep the wheels turning for the same economic system that, according to Shaw's analysis, makes prostitution an inevitability.

Shaw's socialist agenda included a genuine concern for women's rights. His attitude is on occasion unequivocal: 'Unless Woman repudiates her womanliness, her duty to her husband, to her children, to society, to the law, and to everyone but herself, she cannot emancipate herself' (Shaw, 1922, p. 41). He was convinced of the necessity of education and economic independence for women. Yet it must be noted that, in the portrayal of Vivie Warren, the successful achievement of those ends are associated with masculine characteristics not far removed from the travesty of the New Woman in traditionalist anti-feminist satire. This point does not need to be overstressed, but Shaw's attitude towards women's independence is deeply ambivalent and steers an uneasy course between challenging oppressive formations of male authority and conventionally asserting the validity of gender role and biological function. The contradictions of this position are fully apparent in one sentence from *The Quintessence of Ibsenism*: 'The domestic career is no more natural to all women than the military career is to all men; and although in a population emergency it may become necessary for every able-bodied woman to risk her life in childbed just as it might become necessary in a military emergency for every man to risk his life in the battlefield, yet even then it would by no means follow that the child-bearing would endow the mother with domestic aptitudes and capacities as it would endow her with milk' (p. 39). Shaw does not perceive an inevitable conflict between fulfilment and domestic/maternal roles and this is, of course, still an issue of feminist debate. But Shaw's mediation of that position in his plays is, in the context of the construction of gender in Edwardian drama, more problematic than it is in his discursive writing. *Candida* (1900), where domesticity and marriage are central concerns, is a case in point.

The triangle of Morell, Candida, and Marchbanks is superficially reminiscent of Jones's *The Liars* and *The Case of Rebellious Susan*. Yet the intellectual and social milieu of the household of the Christian Socialist clergyman is, as Shaw stresses in the stage directions, miles from Mayfair and St James's, and, whilst Jones's drama implicitly supports domestic ideology, its class structure excluded the actual practicalities of domesticity. Lady Susan and Lady Jessica are divorced from black-leading grates and cleaning boots, but this is central to Candida's experience as Morell's wife.

Dispensing with any intrigue plot, the conflict in *Candida* is an open battle of will for the possession of Candida. In that battle conventional notions of strength and weakness undergo unfamiliar modulations which bring into the central dramatic focus constructs of gender and domestic power relationships of husband/wife and parent/child. These relationships manifest themselves in all the permutations of the triangular situation.

Marchbanks borders on a parody of the effete artist – incompetent in practical and financial matters, socially awkward, horrified by details of mundane reality, physically weak and cowardly. These features are specifically associated with effeminacy. Yet, by a Shavian inversion, he will prove to be the stronger of the two men by the end of the play. In Shaw's examination of domestic and marital structures, the husband is by far the more complex and interesting figure. Morell is as naïve and complacent in his socialism as he is in his domestic arrangement; they constitute the same mind-set. He pompously counsels his curate, 'We have no more right to consume happiness without producing it than to consume wealth without producing it. Get a wife like my Candida; and you'll always be in arrear with your repayment' (Act 1). If the clergyman produces the same amount of happiness as he does wealth, he has a genuine cause to fear Marchbanks' interest in his wife. His complacency is an unthinking and, ultimately, patronizing acceptance of Candida's domestic presence, an exploitation of her wifely support of his public role as political lecturer. It is a role Candida herself willingly accepts just as she invokes the traditionalist view of husband as master. Morell is blind to the actuality of her domestic role, but his ideological position prevents him from subscribing to the direct assertion of his domestic role: 'I dont know of any right that makes me master. I assert no such right' (Act 3). This sounds well, but the play exposes the ways in which the liberal pose covertly and obliquely perpetrates structures of control. He teaches her to think for herself but this only works as long as she thinks the same things he does. His excessive consideration and praise of her elevates her status at the same time as promoting her dependence and asserting her role as ministress of the hearth. But, in their pattern of mutual interdependence, what is exposed by the end of the play is that the promotion of her dependence on him is a function of his dependence on her. *Candida*, Shaw claimed, was 'a counterblast to Ibsen's *Doll's House*, showing that in the real typical doll's house it is the man who is the doll' (Morgan, 1972, p. 65). This is only partly true. Unlike Nora Helmer, Morell would never be able to slam the door and walk out. In spite of his liberal ideological bias, he is fundamentally as confirmed in his acceptance of domestic ideology as the arch conservative.

At the end of the play it is Candida who makes the choice between Morell and Marchbanks. This, however, hardly represents self-determination. The two men tell her she has to choose, and both assume the prerogative of male proprietorship. The only option on offer is for her to belong to one or the other of them. Shaw is, of course, implicated in this as he has created the choice. Morell represents the known and the domestic. Marchbanks inveighs against domestic drudgery, but his assumption that Candida must see matters this way is a misreading of the situation equivalent to Morell's. The play is at its weakest in its presentation of what Marchbanks has to offer positively. It amounts to the empty afflatus of detached Romantic idealism; he wants 'not a scrubbing brush, but a boat: a tiny shallop to sail away in, far from the world, where the marble floors are washed by the rain and dried by the sun; where the south wind dusts the beautiful green and purple carpets. Or a chariot! to carry us up into the sky, where the lamps are stars, and dont need to be filled with paraffin oil every day' (Act 2). If this represents poetic truth, I find it difficult to be much interested in the enigma of the secret in the poet's soul to which Shaw directs us in the final stage direction. But what is more important is that Shaw effectively offers Candida no real alternative at all to remaining within the domestic sphere.

The grounds on which Candida makes her decision, however, lie elsewhere. Through Marchbanks the dominant construct of masculinity is inverted, through Morell subverted. Quite straight-forwardly she chooses the weaker of the two men – Morell. Candida is, throughout the play, a considerably more ambiguous figure than either Marchbanks or her husband. Her motivation and its implications are far more problematic. Her claim that she would give her 'purity and goodness' to Marchbanks 'as willingly as I would give my shawl to a beggar dying of cold' (Act 2) is often taken to be a sign of Candida's liberated and challenging attitude towards conventional codes of female sexual behaviour. But the way it comes across is as that patronizing middle-class charity which is to be bestowed upon the less fortunate. Further, whilst the codes she appears to challenge are inscribed in domestic ideology, what she actually asserts is the primacy, over and above those codes, of the mothering instinct. The problematic issue is that what Shaw mediates as an instinct, her primary instinct, is another of the constructs inscribed in domestic ideology. Candida's eventual self-fulfilment lies in nurturing, but, it must be noted, the nurturing not of children but her grown-up husband. The form her self-assertion takes preserves marital and domestic structures, and conforms to dominant female gender attributes and roles. The intonation is, as in domestic melodrama and the society drama, ennobling sacrifice to those formations which have evolved to make life comfortable for men.

The contradictions in Shaw's treatment of his female characters are exacerbated when they become subject to his concepts of the

Life Force and Creative Evolution. Shaw's views, visionary and optimistic, oppose the pessimism which by the end of the century had become attached to most evolutionary theories and assumptions. Shaw's *a priori* belief in a reasoned and coherent universe results in a rejection of Darwinian theory on the grounds of its pessimism, and its proposal of a mechanistic and accidental version of the evolution of man. The Shavian system presumes the exercise of a universal will which Shaw, translating Bergson's phrase *élan vital*, terms the Life Force. Central to Shaw's belief is that the Life Force is intelligent and benign and that its ultimate aim is the creation through evolutionary process of a being superior to humans. With the coming of the Superman, social, moral, and metaphysical problems will be solved. A sexual conjunction between two individuals could contribute to the eugenic evolutionary process, and the love chase (a convention of romantic comedy adapted in many of Shaw's plays) could be the process of the Life Force in operation. This is comically dramatized in *Man and Superman* (1905).

Jack Tanner preaches Shavian doctrine; Ann Whitefield is its embodiment in action. The play's comic irony is that he is gradually being ensnared by the very force he preaches. No matter how hard he tries to escape, Ann gets her man. Although Tanner is a mouthpiece for the Life Force, many of Tanner's remarks constitute little more than traditionalist bachelor's counsel suffused with sexist gender stereotyping. Ann consequently is persistently represented as a ruthless predator and a threat to male freedom. The ideological implications of this are blurred, and to a certain extent explained away, by the irony and comedy of the play's own genre. Even the interpolation of the Don Juan in Hell sequence, which most explicitly spells out the theory of the Life Force, contributes to the constant undercutting of positions. The lofty debate throws into ironic relief the mundane comedy of the rest of the play, just as the petty but real concerns of the human characters ironically undercut Don Juan's ethereal detachment from reality. Nevertheless, although the play constantly shifts its ground, its ideological implications, as they are part of a wider Shavian system of thought, deserve extrapolation.

In the Epistle Dedicatory to *Man and Superman*, Shaw professes that the effective operation of the Life Force needs rigid sex role divisions. It is the function of man, as thinker and philosopher, to create new mind, it is the function of woman, as mother and childbearer, to create new life. Man's is intellectual activity, woman's is an instinctive regeneration of the race. Women, therefore, are determined by a biological function, men are not. At one level, this is not much more than a version of the construction of gender in society drama (where men have public and women domestic roles) dressed up in a different way. Shaw, however, exalts woman's role. By selecting her mate, she is furthering the eugenic programme of the Life Force and contributing to the advent of the Superman, and, by pursuing her mate, she appears to have the dominant role in sexual relationships. When this is translated into the comico/ironic world of *Man and Superman*, Ann, in accordance with the love chase convention, employs a series of feminine wiles and overcomes a series of obstacles until she fulfils her purpose. The pronouncements of Tanner, the bearer of the duty of intellectual consciousness, are consistently deflated both by Ann and the events of the play. But Tanner still retains a public presence at the end of *Man and Superman*. The comedy of the play asserts Ann's triumph as an agent of the Life Force but at the same time it tends to obscure the fundamental sexism of Shaw's philosophy.

Ann's ruthless pursuit of Tanner is approbated because she seeks not sexual pleasure but motherhood. In effect women's sexuality is denied unless it serves that primary purpose. 'Sexually, Woman is Nature's contrivance for perpetuating its highest achievement' (Act 3). The terminology may differ from the dictum of *The Case of Rebellious Susan*, but the implications do not, where it is said that 'Nature's darling woman is a stay-at-home woman, a woman who wants to be a good wife and a good mother' (Act 3). The underlying premises of arguments diverge, but both are supportive of dominant social and marital structures: 'The Life Force respects marriage only because marriage is a contrivance of its own to secure the greatest number of children and the closest care of them' (Act 3). Shaw arranges a relationship for Ann, as he did for Candida before her, which subserves conventional middle-class codes. Whilst Shaw constructs the hermetic logic of his system, he ignores the fact that marriage is primarily a real social structure. In plays like *Widowers' Houses* and *Mrs Warren's Profession* he castigates marriage for its venality; further, in his analysis of marriage's economic and oppressive formations, his conclusion was that it is effectively a legalized form of prostitution. This analysis sits uneasily with the agenda of the Life Force.

Towards the end of *Man and Superman* Tanner tries to evade his destiny by claiming that Ann's father made him her guardian not her suitor. The following exchange contains a central problem of the theory of the Life Force in that it is both an internal and an external power:

ANN: (*In low siren tones*) He asked me who I would have as my guardian before he made that will. I chose you!
TANNER: The will is yours then! The trap was laid from the beginning.
ANN: (*Concentrating all her magic*) From the beginning – from our childhood – for both of us – by the Life Force. (Act 4)

Women cannot win either way. They are either conscious predatory seductresses or they are mere conduits for a force over which they have no control. Ultimately they have no choice over their social, sexual, or maternal roles. They are driven by a force beyond them to mate appropriately and bear children. The power that the Life Force supposedly gives women merely confirms their oppression. They are circumscribed by a system which confines them to precisely the same sphere of activity as the social and moral codes of the dominant ideology. However, social and economic oppression are susceptible to change and human intervention; the Life Force, conceived of as a universal principle, is not.

Shaw's socialism and his credo of the Life Force share a similar impulse in that they are both comprised of anti-tragic, optimistic, and utopian elements. A common critical stance is to synthesize the two beliefs by seeing them as short-term and long-term strategies. Nevertheless, the two positions exist in exclusive spheres of conceptional reference. Shaw frequently invokes phrases like 'scientific method' or 'scientific natural history' to validate his work over the romantic and sentimental idealism of his fellow dramatists. Whilst the socialist analysis of the economic base of capitalist society may be thus accommodated, the Life Force is neither scientific, natural, nor methodical. It is unempirical, irrational, and mystical. Undershaft in *Major Barbara* (1905) contains both the socialist and the mystical impulses.

The first two acts of *Major Barbara* superficially return to the world of *Widowers' Houses* and *Mrs Warren's Profession*. Undershaft, the millionaire munitions manufacturer, is, like Sartorius and Mrs Warren, dogmatically unashamed of his trade. He also exposes the underlying principles and the ineffectiveness of organizations which aim to mitigate society's brutalities. Barbara, his daughter and Salvation Army major, represents the challenge to this point of view. Like Trench and Vivie, she is confounded by the exposure of the economic basis and political function of what she holds holy. The Army is funded by Bodger the distiller and Undershaft the armourer. Politically it is an agent of social control, inducing humility, guilt, dependence, and subservience on the part of the recipients of its charity and its promises of greater rewards in an afterlife. Barbara's use of religious terminology makes her loss of faith seem more catastrophic than that of either Trench or Vivie. She tells her father, 'I was safe with an infinite wisdom watching me, an army marching to Salvation with me; and in a moment, at a stroke of your pen in a cheque book, I stood alone; and the heavens were empty' (Act 3).

Although socialism is the unspoken remedy for the evils of *Widowers' Houses* and *Mrs Warren's Profession*, there is no internal sense of a remedy for what the characters perceive as insoluble and permanent social and economic structures. Undershaft, however, is 'an instrument of a Will or Life Force' (*B H S*, III, p. 31) and the last act of the play offers a solution. Barbara's spiritual impulse, which mistakenly finds its initial expression with the Salvation Army, is the same as his. More than their literal consanguinity is foregrounded by the syntactical repetition of their exchange at the beginning of their contest to convert each other:

UNDERSHAFT: Where is your shelter?
BARBARA: In West Ham. At the sign of the cross. Ask anybody in Canning Town. Where are your works?
UNDERSHAFT: In Perivale St Andrews. At the sign of the sword. Ask anybody in Europe. (Act 1)

At Perivale, the heavenly city as Cusins calls it, Undershaft is revealed as an iconoclastic paradox − the dealer in death and destruction is the creator of new life. Undershaft caters for the material needs of his workers through social reorganization. Barbara will find her salvation ministering to Perivale's spiritual reorganization.

In the contest for conversion, Barbara cannot win. She is arguing from within an existent 'defective social organization' in which the Salvation Army is fully if helplessly implicated; Undershaft is arguing from a social organization which doesn't exist. The strategy of the utopian vision is one way of ameliorating the ideological problematic of the operation of the Life Force when it appears in what purport to be real social situations. The dream sequence of Don Juan in Hell represents another tactic. The logical conclusion lies in what Raymond Williams has called the 'fantasy of "pure intelligence" ' (p. 286) divorced from any knowable reality of *Back to Methuselah* (1921). The obliteration of social and economic structures, of biological function and sexual difference has its ideological conveniences.

Shaw's work is thoroughly and self-consciously indebted to the traditions and conventions of Victorian and Edwardian drama, yet it is in many respects the most idiosyncratic and iconoclastic. In being so characteristically Shavian, Shaw is probably the least typical of Edwardian dramatists.

Bibliography

The Plays

HENRY ARTHUR JONES
Most of Jones's plays were initially published by Macmillan. His work was also regularly published privately by the Chiswick Press. A four-volume library edition of seventeen plays, *Representative Plays by Henry Arthur Jones*, edited by Clayton Hamilton, was published in 1926 (reprinted St Clair Shores, Mich., 1971). *Plays by Henry Arthur Jones*, a modern edition with textual apparatus edited by Russell Jackson, containing *The Silver King*, *The Case of Rebellious Susan*, and *The Liars* was published in 1986 in the Cambridge University Press series British and American Dramatists 1750–1920.

ARTHUR WING PINERO
Most of Pinero's plays were initially published by Heinemann. A four-volume library edition of eight plays, *The Social Plays of Arthur Wing Pinero*, edited by Clayton Hamilton, was published between 1917 and 1922 (reprinted New York, 1967). *Three Plays* (*The Magistrate*, *The Second Mrs Tanqueray*, and *Trelawny of the 'Wells'*), with an introduction by Stephen Wyatt, was published in 1985 in the Methuen World Dramatists series. *Plays by A. W. Pinero*, edited by George Rowell, containing *The Schoolmistress*, *The Second Mrs Tanqueray*, *Trelawny of the 'Wells'*, and *The Thunderbolt* was published in the Cambridge series in 1986.

JOHN GALSWORTHY
Galsworthy's plays were initially published by Duckworth; his collected plays, *The Plays of John Galsworthy*, was issued in 1929. *Five Plays* (*Strife*, *Justice*, *The Eldest Son*, *The Skin Game*, and *Loyalties*), with an introduction by Benedict Nightingale, was published in the Methuen World Dramatists series in 1984.

HARLEY GRANVILLE BARKER

Most of Granville Barker's plays were initially published by Sidgwick and Jackson. *Three Plays* (1909) contains *The Marrying of Ann Leete*, *The Voysey Inheritance*, and *Waste*; the 1913 reissue contains a revised version of *The Voysey Inheritance*. A more extensively revised version of *The Voysey Inheritance* was published in 1938. A revised edition of *Waste* which amounts to a thorough rewriting of the original play was published in 1927. *The Madras House*, initially published in 1911, also appeared in a revised version in 1925. *Plays by Harley Granville Barker*, edited by Dennis Kennedy, containing *The Marrying of Ann Leete*, *The Voysey Inheritance*, and *Waste* was published in the Cambridge series in 1987. A responsible modern edition containing the textual variants of *The Madras House*, edited by Margery Morgan, was published in 1977 by Methuen.

GEORGE BERNARD SHAW

Shaw's dramatic work was initially published mainly by Constable. The standard library edition of his plays and prefaces is *The Bodley Bernard Shaw: Collected Plays with their Prefaces*, edited by Dan H. Laurence, published in seven volumes between 1970 and 1974. Most of Shaw's plays in reliable texts are published by Penguin.

Selected Secondary Material and Works Cited

Archer, William, *The Old Drama and the New*, London, 1923
– *Real Conversations*, London, 1904
Barker, Harley Granville, 'The Coming of Ibsen', in *The Eighteen-Nineties*, edited by Walter de la Mare, Cambridge, 1930, pp. 159–96
– 'Theatre: Next Phase', *English Review*, 5, 1910, pp. 631–48
Borsa, Mario, *The English Stage of Today*, translated by Selwyn Brinton, London, 1908
Cordell, Richard A., *Henry Arthur Jones and the Modern Drama*, New York, 1932; reprinted New York, 1968
Galsworthy, John, *The Inn of Tranquility*, London, 1912
– *The Works of John Galsworthy*, Manaton Edition, 25 vols, London, 1923–9
– *Letters from John Galsworthy 1900–1932*, edited and with an introduction by Edward Garnett, London, 1934
Henderson, Archibald, *European Dramatists*, London, 1927

Hollege, Julie, *Innocent Flowers: Women in the Edwardian Theatre*, London, 1981

Holroyd, Michael, *The Genius of Shaw*, London, 1979

Howe, P. P., *The Repertory Theatre*, London, 1910

Incorporated Stage Society, *Ten Years 1899–1909*, London, 1909

James, Henry, *The Scenic Art*, edited by Allan Wade, London, 1949

Jones, Doris Arthur, *The Life and Letters of Henry Arthur Jones*, London, 1930

Jones, Henry Arthur, *The Foundations of a National Drama*, London 1913

– *The Renascence of the English Drama*, London, 1895

Kennedy, Dennis, *Granville Barker and the Dream of Theatre*, Cambridge, 1985

Kobbé, Gustav, 'The Plays of Arthur Wing Pinero', *Forum*, 26, 1898, pp. 119–28

MacCarthy, Desmond, *The Court Theatre 1904–1907*, London 1907

McDonald, Jan, *The 'New Drama' 1900–1914*, London, 1986

Macqueen-Pope, Walter, *Carriages at Eleven*, London, 1947; reprinted London, 1972

Mander, Raymond and Mitchenson, Joe, *The Theatres of London*, London, 1963

Marrott, H. V., *The Life and Letters of John Galsworthy*, London, 1935

Mason, A. E. W., *Sir George Alexander and the St James' Theatre*, London, 1935

Morgan, Margery M., *A Drama of Political Man: A Study in the Plays of Harley Granville Barker*, London, 1961

– *The Shavian Playground*, London, 1972

Nicoll, Allardyce, *English Drama 1900–1930*, Cambridge, 1973

– *Late Nineteenth Century Drama 1850–1900*, Cambridge, 1959

Pinero, Arthur Wing, *Robert Louis Stevenson as Dramatist*, with an introduction by Clayton Hamilton, New York, 1914

Purdom, C. B., *Harley Granville Barker: Man of the Theatre, Dramatist and Scholar*, London, 1955

Rowell, George, *Theatre in the Age of Irving*, Oxford, 1981

– *The Victorian Theatre 1792–1914*, second edition, Cambridge, 1978

Shaw, George Bernard, *Bernard Shaw's Letters to Granville Barker*, edited by C. B. Purdom, New York, 1957

– *Collected Letters*, edited by Dan H. Laurence, London, 1965–

– *Our Theatres in the Nineties*, revised edition, 3 vols, London, 1932

– *The Quintessence of Ibsenism*, third edition, London, 1922
– *Selected Non–Dramatic Writing of Bernard Shaw*, edited by Dan H. Laurence, Boston, 1965
Shore, Florence Teignmouth, *Sir Charles Wyndham*, London, 1908
Taylor, John Russell, *The Rise and Fall of the Well-Made Play*, London, 1967
Trewin, J. C., *The Edwardian Theatre*, Oxford, 1976
Trewin, Wendy, *All on Stage: Charles Wyndham and the Alberys*, London, 1980
Weales, Gerald, 'The Edwardian Theater and the Shadow of Shaw', in *Edwardians and Late Victorians*, English Institute Essays 1959, edited by Richard Ellman, New York, 1960, pp. 160–87
Wearing, J. P., *The London Stage 1890–1919*, 6 vols, Metuchen, N. J., 1976–82
Williams, Harold, *Modern English Writers*, London, 1918
Williams, Raymond, *Drama from Ibsen to Brecht*, Harmondsworth, Middlesex, 1973
Wilson, A. E., *Edwardian Theatre*, London, 1951
Woodfield, James, *English Theatre in Transition 1881–1914*, London, 1984

Index